Tales of a First-Year Teacher Sequel:

THE FALL
J.D. Parks

Parks Publishing & Consulting Company, LLC

ISBN -13: 978-1-7326967-4-7

Editing by: Jalesa Parks
Front cover image: Melissa Parks-Dilworth

Print services provided by CreateSpace
United States of America
First printing: November 2019

Published by Parks Publishing & Consulting Company, LLC
P.O. Box 66
Olive Branch, MS 38654

If it be so, our God whom we serve is able to deliver us from the burning fiery furnace, and he will deliver us out of thine hand, O king.

Daniel 3:17

Prologue

Jada had been waiting for this day since the October leaves had begun to fall, and she felt extremely prepared. Clutching the manila folder against her chest, she pictured his expression when she'd allow the printed emails and documents to dramatically fall onto the desk. There was no way the superintendent wouldn't listen to her once he saw them. With a smirk, she pushed open the front office door, and Ms. Allen, the receptionist, offered her a warm smile and a thumbs up. The woman's gesture didn't match the worried look in her eyes, but Jada couldn't let that deter her. She offered a stiff nod in her direction and continued to the larger room. Just before entering, she said a silent prayer: *God, please go with me in this meeting.* She gave the wooden door two firm taps, and it creaked open slowly.

She immediately noticed the tall, red-faced superintendent who she had seen occasionally lounging in the school cafeteria. He murmured a quick greeting before turning his attention back to Mr. Luther, as they continued their small talk about football. Jada waited patiently, allowing herself to wonder about his name. *Judge Luther*, she snorted inwardly. She was still very sure that his Mama didn't give it to him. *If she did, Lucifer would've been a more appropriate choice*, she thought. When their eyes met, the fire and tension that flashed between them was undeniable. He nodded, cupped his hands beneath his chin, and leaned forward on the large, wooden desk. She settled into one of the uncomfortable, straight-back chairs adjacent to his desk and pulled her skirt down snuggly over her knees. She exhaled slowly before opening the folder and folding her hands in her lap. Their talking ceased, and the superintendent turned to her.

"I called this meeting," she started. "Because I wanted to dis—."

"By the way, Luther, what you think about the track team?" Superintendent Greer interrupted before crossing his leg at the ankle and scrolling through his phone. "Oh, I'm sorry, Ms. Harris, you were saying?" He smirked at her, his eyes twinkling devilishly.

Jada looked across the desk and into the eyes of a triumphant Mr. Luther, and she instantly knew that scheduling this meeting had been a huge mistake.

Chapter One

Rihanna crooned loudly from the stereo as Jada parked her car in the crowded parking lot, the air conditioner blowing her freshly pressed hair in different directions. She turned the volume knob while glancing in the rearview mirror, laying each strand of hair back in place and reapplying her mauve-colored lipstick. She scanned the parking lot for familiar cars; they were few and far in between, but she quickly sighted Mr. Williams, the social studies teacher, and Counselor Henson's cars parked side-by-side. Ms. Kimble's black Tahoe wasn't anywhere to be seen. Jada shook her head vigorously as if the memories would simply fall out of her mind. *This is going to be a much better school year*, she thought. There was absolutely no way that things could be as dramatic as they had been last semester, but she still whispered a short prayer.

She couldn't believe it was already August; the sound of her alarm had delivered a swift kick back into reality, and now, as she prepared to exit her car and enter Caldwin High School, she felt drained, yet, satisfied. The summer break had been everything she needed it to be; looking in the mirror now, she could see the bronze glow of her skin as a sure sign of all the days she'd spent in the Atlanta sun with Johnathan.

Just then, her phone buzzed in her lap. She scooped it up and smiled down at Johnathan's text. *I really, really miss you.* She quickly typed back: *You have no idea how much I miss you, Babe.* And she did. She had spent approximately eighty percent of her summer vacation with him, and they had explored so many different art museums, restaurants, and ways to show their attraction to each other without consummating their relationship. And Jada wasn't ashamed that she'd gained more than enough weight to show how happy she was; even Johnathan was plumper than usual.

She remembered their last night together. She had been in her hotel room, making last minute changes to her pacing guide for the upcoming school year when she'd received a text from him that simply said: *I'm falling in love with you, and I want you to know just how much I want you in my life.* The text had caught her off guard because she had just spoken to him twenty minutes ago. Just as she had typed her long reply and her hand hovered over the send button, there was a light tap at the door.

She laid her phone aside and strolled to the door, peering out the peephole at a smiling Johnathan on the other side. She couldn't help the huge smile that spread across her cheeks as she unlocked the door, yanked it open, and rushed into his arms. She barely noticed the Lindt chocolate bouquet in his hands, as she wrapped her arms around his neck and planted a long kiss on his inviting lips. He seemed hesitant at first, attempting to say something, but quickly relaxed before returning her kiss and wrapping both arms about her waist.

He pulled her close and began walking her backwards against her room door. Jada could feel the door against her back as he leaned into her, his lips leaving hers to make a slow trail down her neck. His hands rested atop her round derriere.

The sound of someone clearing his throat saved her, and she looked up to find her next-door neighbor staring back at them in disgust. Jada and Johnathan exchanged heavy looks before chuckling and pushing off the door. Jada grabbed the key from her back pocket and opened the door as Johnathan grabbed the fallen bouquet from the floor and passed his hand over his face. He followed closely behind her, as she entered the room. Inside, he closed the door loudly and grabbed her. She found herself back against the door, his face mere inches from hers.

"So, you plan on finishing what you started?" He stared at her under hooded eyes, his jawbone clenching with what Jada knew was restraint. She knew that if she said the right words she would surely be in trouble. He had made it clear that abstinence was her decision, not his, and if she ever changed her mind, he would be more than happy to oblige.

He began to place kisses along her ear and whispered, "I'll

give you whatever you want. Is this what you want?" He

placed one last kiss on her lips and leaned back to look at her

inquisitively.

Jada's mouth was dry; she knew what she had

promised God, but she, also, knew what her body was saying.

She wanted him bad; she opened her mouth to tell him just

that, but she couldn't seem to get it out.

She sighed heavily, placing both hands on his large

biceps. "I was trying to tell you that I'm falling in love with

you, too." She looked back into his eyes, they were flashing

with passion and temptation. She hoped her eyes weren't

betraying her. "I-I-it---I couldn't find a better way to say it

so—" Her words trailed off, as she peeked back up at him,

not trusting herself enough to look directly into his eyes.

He raised her chin so that she was looking back at

him and spoke softly, "Hey, hey, hey. I'm not complaining."

He tapped her nose lightly. "All men want to be greeted like that. I just thought maybe you wanted something else." He shot her a smooth, tempting look and put his hands behind his back so that she could scan him from head to toe. "And you know, I don't mind delivering." He offered her a hopeful glance.

"Uh uh, Mr. Smooth Deliverer, I didn't order takeout." She pushed her body off the door and stepped around him to put the room key on the kitchen countertop.

He chuckled and stepped behind her, placing his hands on the marble countertop on both sides of her body, locking her in place. "No worries." He kissed her behind her ear. "Have you gotten far with your lesson plans?"

She turned to face him, bracing her hands against his freshly crisped shirt. She had just noticed that he was more dressed up than usual. "I'm very close to the end." She straightened the red tie that was neatly nestled between his muscle-bound pecks. "And why are you so handsome right now? Surely not to sit in my hotel room."

He seemed to suddenly remember why he'd came,

straightening his posture. "Oh, right." He reached for the bouquet of candy sloppily placed on one of the end tables. "I came to take my lady out for a night on the town. Can you come play with me for a few hours?" He gave her a pleading, puppy-dog look while kissing her hand and placing the bouquet on the counter behind her.

"It depends. Does your idea of playing end with my clothes on or off?" She playfully swatted his lips from her hand.

"Hmmm, if I'm being honest, we'd be butt-naked right now, but my plans are very innocent," he chuckled while placing her hand on his chest. He saw the seriousness in her eyes and seemed to sober up immediately. "Look, I told you that I'm willing to go your speed; if you want to wait until the honeymoon, I'm willing to do that. Whatever you want to do. Okay?"

She offered him a huge smile before planting a soft kiss on his cheek. "Well, in that case, yes, I can play."

"Perfect." He playfully slapped her hip and walked

over to plop down on the couch. "Get dressed. Take your time. I'll wait." He nestled both arms behind his head, grinning like the Cheshire cat.

Jada chuckled and walked over to stand in front of him. "Get dressed? What am I supposed to wear?"

He glanced at her standing with her hands on her hip in an over-sized Richard Pryor t-shirt she'd gotten from her ex, Caleb, and a pair of loose pajama shorts. "Look, you could wear what you have on and still be beautiful." He winked at her before placing a pillow behind his head and locking his fingers together over his chest.

She stared back at him pointedly, her hands still fastened on her hips and her eyebrows raised in question.

"Okay," he sighed. "Wear something dressy but casual, no real crazy heels or nothing. I don't need you crying about your feet hurting thirty minutes into the night."

She tossed a pillow in his direction before running to her suitcase. She couldn't imagine what he had planned, and that's what she appreciated about him. Her ex, Caleb, had been so predictable, but Johnathan was a wild card. He was always willing to take risks and try something new, and lately, Jada found herself being the same way. It felt good, freeing, in fact. She sifted through her clothes until she finally found the black, off-the-shoulder romper she had been searching for. She held it up in the light and smiled to herself. *This is it*, she thought. She snatched her wedge sandals from the bottom of the bag and walked towards the bathroom, stopping just long enough to peep out into the living room.

"Give me 30 minutes, Babe." She offered him a sneaky grin.

"Okay." He glanced up at her quickly but then turned to face her when he noticed her facial expression. "Aye, look woman. Don't be trying to give me a heart attack."

"Okay." She loudly hummed Patti LaBelle's "Somebody Loves You, Baby" as she busied herself in the bathroom. Yes, she was ready to play, and she couldn't think of a better person to do it with!

■■■

Forty-five minutes later, she and Johnathan walked arm-in-arm into the brightly lit Atlanta Botanical Garden. The large fountain was surrounded by bright, white lights that bounced off the water in amazing circles that caused Jada's breath to catch in her throat. She stopped abruptly with her hand near her collar bone to take in the scenery. The garden's greenery was shaped into a beautiful, statuesque figure with clear water flowing from her hand. Her tresses were colorful, and the shrubbery gave them an ethnic look that left Jada speechless. Happy with her reaction, Johnathan took her hand and led her down a long walk lined with lights and forest trees, stopping ever-so-often to offer her bits of information about the garden as a historic masterpiece. She listened intently, the soft timber of his voice giving her chills as he recounted each event with pride and admiration.

Finally, they reached an illuminated building that overlooked the garden. Johnathan opened the door and ushered her inside. The chipper hostess asked for his name and promptly showed them to a table near the window. Johnathan pulled out her chair and patiently waited for her to be seated as she scanned the restaurant, her mouth hanging open in awe and her eyes as big as saucers. He settled in the seat across from her, watching her intensely. Jada stared out of the window, watching other couples take the same route they had taken. It was perfect.

She covered Johnathan's hand with her own. "This is so perfect, just beautiful. Thank you."

He nodded, clearly pleased with himself. "A beautiful place for a beautiful woman." He covered her hand with his rather large one, as his lips slid into an easy smile. "These last few months have been amazing. I hadn't dated for a long time before I met you, and now, I'm beginning to see why God wanted me to wait. He was preparing me for you." He reached over and wiped an escaped tear from her cheek and placed a soft kiss on top of her hand.

She peeked at him through lowered eyelashes, just as the waiter came to take their orders. Knowing how indecisive and picky she was, Johnathan ordered four different entrees so that she could taste each one. They ate and discussed everything from their childhood memories to their future goals. She couldn't help but be amazed every time she realized how in sync they were in their careers, their love language, and overall lives. It was as if she had been granted special entry into singer Ciara's head when she prayed to God for Russell Wilson, and now, Jada was sitting across from the man of her dreams, too. Johnathan checked off majority of the boxes that she asked God to fill for her future husband; she just wished that he lived closer. Forcing thoughts of the future out of her head, she gazed back into his intense eyes, shuttering under his sensual stare. She willed thoughts of his body out of her head. *Get it together, girl.* He smiled back at her as if he'd read her mind.

"So, tell me. Did I do good?"

"Good??" She gawked at him in surprise. Surely, he knew that it was the most beautiful evening she had ever experienced.

"Maybe one day I'll be able to show you just how *good* you did." She winked at him over her wine glass.

Now, fussing with her hair, she hated the summer had to come to an end, but more importantly, she hated that it would be two weeks before she'd see Johnathan again. However, considering all of the new cars in the school parking lot, she knew his visit was one of the only things that would get her through the first few days of classes.

Chapter Two

"Everyone, please be seated." The man's baldhead shined brightly under the library's florescent lights. He stood near the front desk with his hands linked in front of his flat torso. "I'd like to welcome you all back for another school year at Caldwin; I am Judge Luther, the new head principal here."

"Judge Luther? Is that his real name?" Mrs. Inglewood asked, while snickering softly.

"Girl, I sure hope not," Ms. Henson answered while shaking her head.

"Now," the principal continued, "I'm sure you're wondering if that's my real name." He chuckled while looking around the room as heads nodded. "The answer is yes. My mother gave me that name because she thought I'd grow up to be a law man, but clearly, that didn't work out." He glanced from table to table before grabbing the small remote from the librarian's desk. "But we're not here for me, or for you; we're here for these students. Still, you probably want to know more about me. I have been in education for forty plus years, and I've held every position possible within the school system, teacher, board member, superintendent, principal, and retired principal." He laughed again. "The only one I failed at was the retired part because now, I'm back in a principal position. But I want you all to understand that my main priority is the students. I'd like for you to turn your attention to the projector." The screen began to lower, and a picture of a white woman with blonde hair and red lipstick popped up on the screen.

"This," he boomed loudly, "is Jewel Payne, an education guru who helps teachers and people to better understand the effects of poverty on school-aged children. I think it's extremely important for us to keep the poverty-stricken environment of this community in mind as we work to educate our students so that we always remember why underprivileged students cannot learn. Over the course of this year, we will use her work as a foundational framework for getting our students where we need them to be." He silently stared at each table before grabbing a stack of papers from the table beside him.

Jada looked around the room to see if anyone else felt as uneasy as she did. Yes, they served an under-privileged population of children, but to say that they would be unable to learn seemed to negate the very reason she had decided to work at Caldwin High School. She hoped that he meant that the students had difficulty learning or needed additional assistance. Either way, she planned to give him the benefit of the doubt; after all, he did come out of retirement.

"Now, I'm passing out contact information for the school administration. Let me introduce you to your new assistant principals. First, we have Mr. Fulton," Principal

Luther waved his hand towards the round table closest to the library entrance. A very tall and brown-skinned man with curly brown hair stood and crossed his hands at the waist.

Loudly, he barked, "Good morning, family!"

A chorus of "good mornings" sounded around the room.

"Girl—." Mrs. Inglewood whispered, rolling her eyes and staring at Jada goofily.

Jada attempted to avoid making eye contact, stifling a chuckle that was fighting to break free from the pits of her stomach. She bit the corner of her lip to keep it down.

"What is this?" Mrs. Inglewood continued. "We done left for summer break and came back to the circus. Why that man so loud? And them curls? Jeeesuus," she whispered, nudging Ms. Henson, the counselor, as she talked.

"Look, I can't be in no more drama like last year. Behave," Ms. Henson warned, swatting at her elbow. "Everybody already looks at me like the school-tramp-of-the-year." An expression of sadness passed over her face and left her lips in a pout.

Jada agreed silently. She and Ms. Henson were on much better terms since she'd found out about the counselor's affair with the married, former assistant principal. She knew that Ashton's sudden death had managed to alleviate some of the animosity. Still, Jada planned to keep her distance. New principals meant new possibilities for scandal, and she couldn't say that the counselor wouldn't take a gamble at it.

Mr. Fulton's voice broke into her thoughts, "It's an honor to be here! We're gonna have a wonderfully, marvelous school year filled with plentiful learning and good times. Ain't that right?!" He looked around the room expectantly; the room was silent. "Uh, uh. We can't have that! I *said* that we gon' have a good school year! Ain't that right?!"

"That's right!" A few of the teachers yelled in response.

Jada lowered her head and chuckled to herself. He

reminded her of Eriq La Salle from the movie *Coming to America*; his hair was shiny and curly as if he had just emptied a bottle of Soul Glow over the top of his head. He just seemed so different from other principals she had met before. She didn't quite know what to make of him.

"That's what I like to hear!" He clapped his hands together loudly. "Now, I will be over discipline here, so if you have any problems with student behavior, bring them to me expeditiously." He settled back in his seat, his knees seeming mere inches from his chest.

"Thank you, Mr. Fulton," Principal Luther said, rubbing his hands together.

Jada noticed that the assistant principal didn't acknowledge him in return, which seemed odd, but she shrugged it off as just one of those men things.

"Next," Mr. Luther continued. "I'd like to introduce you to assistant principal Calloway. Those of you who were here last year know her."

Jada watched in utter disbelief as Ms. Calloway stood

slowly and stared down each table; her lips spread into a slight grin when her eyes landed on Jada. Jada recognized challenge in her eyes and hoped that her own eyes made it clear that she was more than up for it.

"Thank you, Mr. Luther," the woman replied in a deep voice. "I'm happy to be back again. This time as an assistant principal." She stared at Jada pointedly. "My title has changed, but my job has not. I will still be in charge of instruction, so I'll be helping you all with curriculum and lesson plans."

"As *if* she did that last year," Jada found herself mumbling.

"What you say?" Ms. Henson asked, anxious to know what she'd whispered.

"Oh, nothing." Jada wasn't a fool; she knew that Ms. Henson and Ms. Calloway ran in the same circle. There was no way she would get herself caught up in drama this early in the school year.

Mr. Luther walked back to the front of the room.

"Thank you, APs. At this time, I'm going to release each of you to go work in your classrooms until lunch. I ask that during lunch, those of you who are returning teachers, please grab one or two of the new teachers and help them get adjusted to Caldwin. We will meet back here in the library after lunch."

That's it? Jada thought, looking around the room. Being that it was the beginning of the school year, Jada expected much more information and guidance. Even though she felt that last semester had given her a wealth of knowledge, in some ways she still felt unprepared, especially with her move from teaching ninth graders to seniors. She assumed her new position would be similar to teaching college students, but many people had warned her that her expectations were far too high. She spotted a pair of new faces sitting at one of the tables in the far corner of the room. Grabbing her belongings, she made a beeline for the two women.

"Hi, I'm Ms. Harris," she offered cheerfully,

extending her hand to one woman and then the other.

"Hi, I'm Mrs. Glenn," the younger woman answered. Her eyes shifted nervously from the door to Jada. She looked to be no older than forty, but with her choppy brown bangs, shoulder length hair, and rosy red cheeks, she had a girlish quality, which worried Jada. She spoke very timidly, and Jada knew that the students would quickly notice her nervous energy and use it against her if she didn't develop a backbone within the next two days.

"And I'm Mrs. Kadashe." The older woman accepted Jada's hand and shook it softly. She, too, seemed out of her element, often fiddling with her short blonde hair. She looked to be in her early fifties. "We're both in the English department," she offered.

"Oh, great. I am, too." Jada smiled and settled into a seat across from them. "I teach the seniors."

"Oh, my God. You look so young," Mrs. Glenn said, staring at Jada closely. "I-I'll be teaching the sophomores, and Mrs. Kadashe will be teaching the creative writing class."

"Nice." Jada glanced at her watch. "I know you all probably aren't familiar with the community, so perhaps we can meet up for lunch, and I can fill you in on what to expect here."

"How nice!" Mrs. Kadashe exclaimed. "That would be great. We'll meet you here at noon."

"That works for me! See you in a little while." Jada waved a quick goodbye and exited the library, running into a speeding Mr. Williams.

He grabbed her elbow, helping her to steady her balance. "Why, look who it is! I just came from your classroom looking for you, girl!" He enveloped her in a tight hug.

Considering that Jada hadn't spoken to him all summer, she was unprepared for such a warm greeting. They hadn't spoken since she'd confronted Ms. Henson about her and Mr. William's scheme to uproot the former assistant principal from his position, but she was willing to follow his lead.

"Hey!" She exclaimed, pulling out of the odd embrace. "What did you need?"

"Oh, nothing, honey. I was just going to say hello and catch up with you. How was your summer?" He stared at her intensely, anticipating her response.

"It was absolutely amazing. I hated for it to end!" She drawled. They walked side-by-side towards her classroom.

"Amazing, huh? Sounds like you done got you a man!" He wriggled his glasses, crossed his arms over his chest, and dramatically scanned her from head to toe.

She slapped his elbow playfully. "Something like that."

"Oooo, is he from Michelin?"

"Oh, no he's an art teacher in Atlanta."

"Wait, girl." He stopped her in her tracks. "His name ain't Joshua is it?" He looked genuinely concerned.

"Oh, no." Her heart seemed to settle its fast pace.

"Chiiiild. I was about to say that we got the same

taste in men." He pinched her elbow. "But I'm so happy for you. You're glowing."

"Aww, am I? Thanks." She placed her hands on both cheeks, hoping to ease the schoolgirl smile that had spread across her face. "You had a good summer?"

"Yes ma'am. I got a new beau who is absolutely charming, got that savage, hood thing going on, too. And can cook! Oh, my God. He's everything a man and most women," he whispered, "could hope for."

"Look who's glowing now!" She quipped, flicking his arm lightly.

"Yeah, yeah. Well, it's so good to see you. This is gonna be a great year." He hugged her quickly and began a brisk walk back towards his classroom.

A feeling of enthusiasm spread throughout Jada's body. She had been dreading her return because she wasn't sure what things would be like between her, Ms. Henson, and Mr. Williams, but now she realized that everyone was ready to move on and forget all that had occurred last semester.

And with the former principals and Mrs. Kimble gone, it wouldn't be hard after all. Pulling her key out of her tote, she opened her classroom door and stepped inside. The floor sparkled with a new coat of wax, and the dry erase boards gleamed with a freshly cleaned shine.

"Hey, youngin'!" Mr. Oliver, the janitor exclaimed, stopping in her doorway and tipping his hat in her direction. "You glad to be back?"

"Oh, yes sir," Jada beamed. "Very happy to be back."

Chapter Three

"I used to teach online classes in Michigan, and *that* was a monster!" Mrs. Glenn exclaimed. It was the first time that Jada had heard her voice raise above a whisper; the sudden shift had startled her. But even then, Jada didn't miss what she'd said. If she thought online classes were troublesome, she couldn't possibly be prepared for the students at Caldwin.

"You've never taught in a traditional classroom before?" Jada asked, stabbing a piece of chicken on her plate.

"No, but it can't be much different." The woman shrugged her shoulders and took a small bite of her kosher salad. "But I am worried that I haven't received much guidance in the instructional department. I'm not exactly sure what Ms. Calloway expects from incoming teachers."

"Oh, I'm the leader for our department so I'm sure that I can help you with that. I strongly suggest that you write up a thorough pacing guide for the school year and lesson plans for at least the first month." Jada offered her a reassuring smile.

"A p-pacing guide?" Mrs. Kadashe asked, concerned lines sketched in her forehead.

Jada looked from one woman to the other. They both looked slightly confused. "Umm, yeah. It's like a syllabus, or a plan for the whole school year. It maps out each unit and area you plan to cover by dates, but it's not as detailed as weekly lesson plans."

"Oh, so like a playbook?" Mrs. Kadashe asked, wrapping a slice of lettuce around a chicken tender. "I can do that."

"Who checks the pacing guide and lesson plans?" Mrs. Glenn asked, small pieces of food flying from her mouth.

Jada leaned back in her chair. "Well, Ms. Calloway is supposed to; I'm not sure if she will, but you can definitely bring them to me, and I will check them and give you feedback."

"No offense, but aren't you a little young to be the department leader?" Mrs. Kadashe looked at her over lowered glasses.

"To some, yeah. But Mr. Jackson thought I would be perfect for it."

"He was the old principal, right?"

"Yeah."

"Why'd he leave? I've heard some pretty good things about him from other teachers." Mrs. Kadashe sprinkled salt on some cucumber slices and stuffed them in her mouth.

Jada wasn't expecting the question, but she didn't feel like she needed to give them every detail. "He just made some poor decisions."

"Must've been some pretty bad decisions," Mrs. Glenn whispered. "So, w-w-what are the students like?"

"They're great kids, lively and comical, but strong-willed. You definitely need a backbone."

"I got that as a flight attendant," Mrs. Kadashe offered absentmindedly. "Ever had to stuff a passenger's carry-on in an overhead bin? That takes backbone," she quipped.

"You've never taught before?" Jada asked, one eyebrow raised.

"Oh, no," the woman chuckled. "I'm really just trying to be home with my son; he's a freshman at Michelin High school. Being that he's just now entering high school, I felt like I needed to be at home more. I lucked up and found a job at Caldwin."

"Wait, your son doesn't attend Caldwin?" Jada didn't believe what she was hearing. She hated to judge, but it didn't seem like Mrs. Kadashe was here for the right reasons. She couldn't foresee her being at Caldwin long; the students could sense inauthenticity from a mile away.

"Oh, no. I would never let my son go to *this* school." She sipped from her iced tea. "The teacher and principal turnover rates are appalling. Plus, the test scores are very low. Heck, I wouldn't even be here myself if I'd received a better job offer elsewhere."

"Oh, wow," Jada murmured. "And what about you, Mrs. Glenn?"

"I wanted to work in Michelin High School, too, but the job listings were scarce. My husband, two kids, and I just moved down from a small suburb in Michigan. I'm a former librarian."

Hmph, that explains a lot, Jada thought. "Oh, okay. So, this will be an entirely new experience for both of you." Jada pushed the remaining food around on her plate. She had lost her appetite. "The best piece of advice I can give you, because I learned it last semester, is to make sure that you get to know your students. It will really help you going forward. Oh, and be consistent with your rules. Set the rules on day one and stick to them." She glanced back and forth from each woman.

Mrs. Kadashe cleared her throat. "And when did you start teaching at Caldwin?"

Jada sensed an attitude but chose to ignore it. "January of the last school year," she said. "So only a few months actually."

"Hmm, well it's close to one o'clock." The woman glanced at her watch. "We should probably be getting back."

Jada knew when she was being dismissed; she found herself chuckling inwardly because she remembered when she had once been a know-it-all teacher, too; however, the students had quickly changed that and influenced her in ways that she hadn't been prepared. She knew that the same would happen for these two; she just prayed it wouldn't break them. She gathered her belongings, wished both ladies good luck, and hopped into her gold PT Cruiser.

∎∎

"Please take a piece of white paper from the middle of your table," Mr. Luther said. "Draw four quadrants, and in each box, write one word that describes the students we serve here." Jada complied, writing the words: *lovable, insecure, outspoken,* and *underestimated* in one of the four boxes.

"Now," he continued, "I'd like for you to discuss your responses with the people at your table." A number of hands shot up in the air.

"Yes, Mrs. Kadashe," he called.

"I'm not sure how I can write words to describe them if I don't know much about them." Other new teachers murmured their agreement and lowered their hands.

"Well, that is a problem. So, here is a chance for you to get to know them from other people in the room." He returned his attention back to the assistant principals before looking back up over his glasses and saying, "Please proceed with your discussions."

Mrs. Kadashe cleared her throat loudly. "I mean, I get that, but we can't solely depend on other teachers' perceptions of these kids. Will we have a new teacher's orientation or something?" Jada could tell that she was frustrated from the streaks of color that had risen in her pale cheeks.

Mr. Luther rose suddenly from his seat. "Excuse me, excuse me. Let me have all of your attention." He removed his glasses as the crowd quieted. "Right now, all I want you to do is discuss and learn from each other. I know what I'm doing. I've been doing this for years, Mrs. Kadashe. All of your concerns will be addressed." He placed his spectacles back on top of his nose and pushed them up before returning to his seat.

Jada and Mr. Williams exchanged glances from across the room. She could tell from the side glances that Mrs. Kadashe threw in Mr. Luther's direction that she wasn't satisfied with his response, and it seemed that the rest of the new teachers were on the same page. They looked lost and utterly confused; Jada wondered if she had looked the same way. Even more, she wondered if anyone, other than her, noticed their level of discomfort. For a small amount of time she had felt like she was drowning when she first started teaching at Caldwin, and no one really seemed concerned. But there was nothing she could do to help these teachers. Because she was still fairly new herself, she knew they wouldn't listen to her. She turned her attention back to her group.

"So, how are we doing over here, guys?" Ms. Calloway asked, taking a seat at Jada's table.

Ms. Henson answered dryly. "We're good. You know we know these kids."

"Well, you might, but Ms. Harris here is still in her first year. People tend to forget that she's still a newbie." Ms. Calloway flashed a fake smile in Jada's direction.

"Well, you know, I experienced so much scandal and witnessed so many people not doing their jobs that I feel like I've been here longer than five months." Jada returned her fake smile, wiping invisible crumbs from her shirt. "Based on the criteria here, I may be assistant principal in the next few months. Who knows?" Jada chuckled softly and shrugged, staring back at Ms. Calloway pointedly.

There was a flicker of anger in the woman's eyes as she looked back at Jada.

"Well, thank God that I'm here to show you how it's done!" The woman said through clenched teeth. She stared back at Jada before flouncing to a table of new teachers.

Jada rolled her eyes and folded her arms, catching Ms. Henson chuckling to herself. Now that Ms. Calloway had a more powerful position, Jada knew that they would have many more encounters that would certainly test her patience. She wanted to say that she was more than ready for it, but she couldn't.

Chapter Four

No, it can't be…. Jada thought, rubbing her eyes and blinking three times before looking back at the approaching form. She was sure that she was tired or delusional because the person walking towards her looked oddly familiar. She squinted harder. *Yes, it is her*, she thought.

The girl's hips swayed slowly from side to side as she approached Jada. "Hi, Ms. Harris." The girl's eyes lowered to the floor shyly before looking back up at Jada expectantly.

"V-Vanessa?"

A large smile spread across the girl's face. "Yes, ma'am. How are you?"

"I-I. It's so good to see you." Jada opened her arms,

and the girl quickly fell into them, lightly resting her head on Jada's shoulder. "You had us worried about you. How are you?"

The girl stepped back, still holding Jada's hand. "I'm okay." Jada caught the flash of sadness in her eyes. "I-I lost the baby." Her eyes remained fastened to the floor as she shifted her weight from foot to foot.

"Oh, I'm so sorry." Jada rubbed her arm lightly, hoping it would give her some sense of comfort. She couldn't imagine being sixteen and losing a baby and having to return to the very high school where it all started. She knew the students would be talking about Vanessa's sudden return. Quite frankly, Jada was surprised to see her, too. She was even more curious to know what had become of Coach Young. As far as Jada knew, he was working at a small school in Alabama, but no one seemed to know what had transpired between he and Vanessa. Seeing the girl now, Jada could tell that the relationship hadn't been kind to her.

Jada locked arms with the girl and steered her

towards her classroom. "So, what's your schedule looking like?"

Vanessa seemed to heave a sigh of relief at the change of subject. "I'm back in your English class." She smiled back at Jada.

"Well, I'm actually not teaching freshman English this year. I'm with the seniors now." Jada squeezed her arm.

"T-the seniors?" The girl looked defeated once again. "I really wanted to be in your class, Ms. Harris. E-everyone's gonna be talking and stuff," she pouted.

"You can't worry about that. Look, I can talk to your teacher if you want me to." They stopped just shy of Jada's classroom door. "I'll tell him to watch out for you."

"Y-yeah, that'll be good."

"Okay, his class is right beside mine. If you need anything or just want to talk, you always know where to find me."

"O-okay. Thanks." Vanessa sauntered into the room, with Jada close behind her. All the students' eyes turned and followed the girl to her seat, and their murmurs became small whispers. Vanessa was right; they were already speculating. Jada made her way to Mr. Keystone, who was more than willing to keep the student gossip at bay.

Walking out, Jada turned to look in Vanessa's direction. The girl looked back at her with pleading eyes. Jada winked, and the look of worry seemed to ease slightly. For the first time, Jada wished that she was teaching freshman English again, but walking into her classroom with all her new students, she was excited to see what this year would bring.

"Ladies and Gentlemen, welcome back. I am Ms. Harris, and this is English IV." She smiled at them as she gathered the stack of syllabi from her desk. "Until I learn your names, you all will sit in assigned seats. Once I learn them, you can sit wherever you'd like." The familiar sound of groans filled the room causing Jada to chuckle inwardly. "Oh, you guys pout like the freshman!"

"Assigned seats? You know how long it's been since

we had assigned seats?" One boy chimed in. "You trippin'."

"Oh, I don't remember falling." Jada looked down at the floor sarcastically.

The boy stared back at her in confusion. "Falling? What you talkin' bout?"

"Well, you said I was trippin'. I'm trying to remember when exactly I fell. That *is* what *tripping* means."

"Oh, mane, she gotta smart mouth." He slapped the hands of a boy sitting next to him, both sporting ombre blonde box fades with identical parts on the left side. "She must ain't met our class befo'." He smirked at Jada while lounging lazily in his desk.

Jada knew a challenge when she saw one; she figured she'd play along. "No, I haven't met you before, sir. Tell me your name."

"I'm Adrian, but everybody call me Wooda."

Jada cocked her head to the side, frown lines sketched in her forehead. "Wooda? Where'd that come from?"

"Sh—, you want my whole family tree or sum'?

Folks just call me that. *You* can call me Adrian."

"Hmm, Adrian is fine with m—," Jada started, just as a loud knock sounded on her door. She looked through the rectangular glass to see Coach Lewis staring back at her, his fake tooth glistening like always. His sly grin was one she most definitely did not miss, and she had to admit that when she didn't see him at the professional development meeting, she'd been overjoyed. But, it was all for naught because here he was looking at her as if she were prime rib. She pulled the door open slowly.

"Hey there, pretty lady," he said, sucking his teeth, looking her up and down, and resting his hand against the door frame.

"Hi, Coach Lewis." She ignored his gaze. "Do you have the modified class rosters?"

"Naw, they still working on 'em; so, you gon' have to hold first period for a while until they get everything figured out."

"What do you mean 'figured out'? Did we not have

the whole summer?" She blew out an exasperated breath. She'd known when she first got to the school that majority of the students only had two classes on their schedule, but the sight of Vanessa had clouded her thoughts. She hated that Coach Lewis had been the one to darken her door with the reminder.

"So, how long are we talking?" She asked, refusing to look him in the eye. She knew her face would tell him just how disgusting she found him; ever since he'd made the snide remarks about Vanessa *wanting* Coach Young's attention and his refusal to help Jada challenge Ashton's expulsion, she had lost the little respect for him that she had. She partly held him responsible for Ashton's death. When she looked at him, she saw nothing but a coward and a pervert.

"First period will probably be in your class for half the day." He stepped back and crossed his arm over his large chest. He was definitely taller and bulkier than most men in the school, not very different from a modern-day Mr. T.

Her eyes must've bulged out of her head. "Half the day?! Woooow." She began to bite her lower lip.

"Oh, no. I know Ms. Teach Bell-to-Bell ain't worried!" He mocked. "I'll let you know when they decide to switch classes. Til' then, have fun." He blew the whistle hanging around his neck and jogged down the hall, seemingly pleased with himself for delivering the worst news she could've heard all day.

Closing the door, she turned back to the students who had taken the opportunity to whip out their phones and talk loudly to each other.

"So, you got us til' lunch, huh? Ain't no different from the first day of class every year." Adrian smirked at her. "Boooy, you gon' hate our class."

Satan, you sure know how to play one heck of a cruel joke, Jada thought. "Okay, everyone, like I was saying, you're going to be in assigned seats. I'm going to pass around a piece of paper, and I'd like for all of you to write your names."

Got you, she thought while smiling at a slouching Adrian as he wrote his name on the top line of the paper before turning around, mumbling a few words to the student behind him, and passing the paper. Jada had no idea what she would do with these students for the next five hours, but she had to think of something fast. It was bad enough that she had fifty students scrunched into such a tiny space; she'd had to ask Mr. Oliver to bring extra desks from the supply closet, which he hadn't been very happy about. On top of that, she didn't know any of their names. She couldn't log into the data system and print a roster, and even if she could, it would be unreliable at this point.

A student sitting in the front desk on the last row waved the piece of paper in the air, and Jada quickly walked over to retrieve it. The room sounded with boisterous laughter as her eyes fixated on fifty printed signatures, all of which read *Adrian Chambers*. She could barely contain her frustration and humiliation when she looked in Adrian's direction, a smug smile tugging at the corners of his mouth.

"I told you that you were gonna hate us." He placed his thumb and forefinger on the side of his forehead, pure cockiness and satisfaction written on his face. Jada knew she had to play it cool; otherwise, he'd know that he'd gotten the best of her.

She folded the paper in half and burst into loud laughter. And she laughed. And when they looked at her inquisitively and then afraid, she laughed even more, until tears were streaming down her face. The room was silent as she chuckled to herself. "You know, this was ingenious. Here's the thing, I don't need to know your names to put you in assigned seats." She walked over to the podium. "As soon as you all realize that I am not here to harm you or even go back and forth with you, the better off we'll all be. But until then, I will play along. So, here it is. Since you obviously did not want to give me your names, I will assign you names and seats, starting with you, Adrian. You will be in the first seat of row one, and since I know your name, you can keep it. Please move now."

He stared back at her as if he had seen a ghost before grabbing his empty backpack and grumbling, "Ole girl crazy."

Jada stifled a chuckle and pointed to a young girl in the back. "You will sit after Adrian. Your name will be Marian Wright Edelman." Jada began to draw a seating chart on a piece of copy paper, writing the assigned name in each box.

A look of confusion passed across the girl's face as she snatched up her belongings and made her way to the desk. "Who dat anyway?" She stared back at Jada in puzzlement.

"Marian Wright Edelman?" Jada asked. "That's a wonderful question, and that's exactly what you're going to spend some time finding out after I assign everyone else and go over the class syllabus."

The class groaned loudly.

"Oh, no, we're not groaning are we? Isn't it important to know who each of you have become?" Jada laughed hysterically as she watched them exchange glances and

slouch in defeat. Even Adrian wasn't smiling anymore.

Chapter Five

The boy smiled down at Jada, as she carried her tray of Salisbury steak, potatoes, and a roll to one of the lunchroom's longest tables. Looking up, she smiled back at Ashton. She'd been pleasantly surprised when she'd seen his large photo hanging high in the lunchroom with the caption: *Never Gone, Always in Our Hearts*. It had been a kind gesture petitioned by the students, and she'd been even more pleased when the new principals had granted the students' wish. Ever so often, she saw students standing under the picture with their heads bowed and one hand over their hearts, and at other times, she'd even heard students cracking jokes and saying, "Ashton would've fell out his chair at that one." Even Jada found herself thinking about Ashton and how he would've laughed at different situations.

"So, that kid was a gang banger, right?" Mrs. Kadashe plopped her tray down on the table, startling Jada and instantly pulling her out of her thoughts.

"What kid?" Jada asked, slicing into the steak.

"The one on the wall. I heard he was selling drugs and stuff."

Jada's fork and knife clanged to the tray. "I'm not sure who told you that, but Ashton was not a gang banger." She stared the woman squarely in her eyes.

"I mean, he was killed, right?" The woman cut into her steak and plopped a cube in her mouth.

"Yes, he was. Brutally. But you should refrain from speaking on delicate subjects, especially when you don't have all the facts." Jada wiped the side of her mouth with a napkin.

"Whoa, I didn't mean any harm. I'm just trying to figure out what happened." The woman scooped a spoonful of peas in her mouth. "I mean, I'm new, and half of these kids seem like gang bangers."

Jada had heard enough. "Which students are you referring to? Surely not the white ones. I don't understand how the term gang bangers has become so loosely associated with Black students. You didn't say he must've been mischievous or a class clown. You didn't say that about any of them. You immediately assumed that they were these barbaric gang bangers who just so happen to show up for school."

"Well, I didn't mean it like that. Just being honest, the white students don't give me very much trouble. It's the Black students who disrupt my class the most."

"Oh, wow, what a surprise!" Jada whispered sarcastically. "You just referred to some of their closest friend as a gang banger without taking the time to even ask about him." She turned to fully face the reddening woman. "Have you even asked the students about him?" The woman's downcast eyes answered for her. "Wait. Have you even asked the students about themselves?" Once again, Mrs. Kadashe's eyes betrayed her. "Hmph. And you somehow managed to arrive at the conclusion that they were gang bangers. Boy, that's beyond disgusting." Jada stood slowly, grabbed her tray, and marched to the teacher's lounge. She couldn't stand to be next to the woman one second longer.

She wished she'd told her that Ashton was a star athlete who never missed practice, an honor roll student, and a prospective member of the National Beta Club, but she couldn't say that any of that information would've made much of a difference. People like Mrs. Kadashe hadn't socialized with people of color and if she had, she must've been in a superior position because she simply hadn't tried to get to know the students. Jada was aware that the administrators had been called to her classroom every day since school started a week ago, and considering their conversation, Jada knew why the students were giving her such a hard time.

Jada looked down at her shrunken steak, assuming

that by now it was too cold to eat. She sent Johnathan a quick message: *These new teachers are the worst ☹ Help!* She was surprised at how quickly her phone sounded, letting her know she had an incoming message.

It was from Johnathan: *Uh oh, someone's gotten under your skin. Think about this, though. Someone probably sent the same message about you when you first started. ☺*

Jada hadn't considered that, but he was right. *Why do you always have to give people the benefit of the doubt?* She responded.

He replied back, *Because, sometimes, if you don't, who will? Shake it off. Talk to you after work.*

Jada started to reply back but changed her mind. This was one of the things that she both liked and disliked about him. He had this coolness about him that made him an instant mediator and likable to almost everyone he met, but sometimes, Jada wanted him to hear her all the way out, to kick up a little dust with her. However, he was always preaching about positive energy and clearing your aura, all of which she understood, but some situations warranted a response, right?

Dumping the cold food into the garbage can, she walked towards the lunchroom to return her tray. Mrs. Kadashe's eyes met hers, and she read an apology in them. She nodded stiffly in acknowledgment before dropping her tray in one of the plastic bins filled with water. *Maybe Johnathan was right*, she thought.

■■

"Okay, ladies and gentlemen, last night you were asked to read Graham Greene's "The Destructors". How many of you actually read it?" Jada watched as roughly ten of the thirty students' hands raised high in the air. "Hmmm, so that means that the rest of you didn't read, and you definitely missed a treat." She made it a point to smile at each student as she shuffled over to the podium to jot down a quick note to call parents this week. Other than a few students in each class, she hadn't experienced too many behavioral incidents. After spending five hours with her the first week, her first period class had gotten the memo and quickly spread the word that she was 'super crazy' to the rest of her classes. Even Adrian was calmer; her new problem was that no matter how she tried, she couldn't get the students to complete homework reading assignments. Their failing quiz grades didn't seem to bother them, and they simply shrugged when questioned about it. She had to do something; otherwise, it was going to be a tough six weeks.

"I'd like for you all to grab your textbooks and turn to "The Destructors." As the students noisily turned to the story, Jada grabbed a blue choir robe from the closet at the front of the classroom. She'd approached Mrs. Eloise, the choir director, two weeks ago about borrowing a robe. Thirty-five pairs of eyes looked at Jada in confusion. It always made Jada feel accomplished to see the students' interest piqued, but it also prompted the greatest challenge. The hard part wasn't getting their attention, it was keeping it that required true talent.

"The great philosopher Tupac said, 'Only God can

judge me.' Raise your hand if you believe that." She looked about the room. All the students raised their hands. Jada continued, "I figured you all would think that." She pulled a wooden gavel and tablecloth from behind the podium, dragged an empty desk to the front of the class, draped the tablecloth on the desk, and placed the gavel on top. "Now, you all agreed with Tupac, but what if judgment was placed in your hands?"

With his eyebrow raised, Adrian asked, "Whatchu' mean by that?"

"What I mean, Adrian is—," Jada leaned against the podium and crossed her arms over her chest. "What if you were given the opportunity to judge someone for their wrongdoing? Would you take it?"

"Fa sho," he snarled. "I'd get them fools that smoked my cousin Ashton." Jada found herself startled by his matter-of-fact tone and the new revelation that he and Ashton were relatives. It was the first piece of personal information he'd offered.

Jada's eyes glistened with sorrow. "I'm sorry, Adrian. I didn't know."

"It ain't no thing," he said, waving off her sentiment and slouching more in his seat.

"I'm sure that many of you would go after Ashton's killer, right?" She scanned the room, as majority of the students nodded their heads in agreement. "I thought so. Judgment is the topic of today's class and last night's homework reading. "The Destructors" refers to a gang of teenage boys who decide to destroy the home of an old man. The problem, though, is that we don't know what wrong the old man committed against the boys. So, you guys will be the judge."

Jada pointed to the directions already listed on the board as she spoke. "I'd like for you to silently read page 112, which gives you descriptions of each boy in the gang. I'm going to pass out an organizer, and I'd like for you to first characterize and then, evaluate, or give your honest opinions of each boy. Once you are finished, I'd like for you to go to the actual scene of the crime on page 116 and determine who is at fault, then we're going to have a live court trial right here in class."

Jarvis, who typically remained silent during every class session, raised his hand. With Jada's acknowledgment, he asked, "Can I be the judge?"

Jada smiled, "Certainly. Here's your robe." She draped the long cloth across his desk.

Irene raised her hand high. "And I'll be the defense attorney."

Dorian spoke loudly, "Aye. I wanted to be the defense attorney!"

"Guess you gotta be the other one," Irene retorted, grabbing one of the extended bow ties.

"Dang. I guess I'll be the other lawyer, Ms. Harris." He shot Irene a goofy grin. "Wait 'til I make my case. I'ma eat you up in court." He grabbed the other bow tie from Jada.

"Boy, please," Irene spat. "You didn't even read the story last night. Good luck tryna get all the facts now." She buried her head in the book while writing vigorously on the organizer handout.

"Yeah, yeah, we'll see." Dorian commenced to read, placing his headphones over his ears as he worked.

"Ladies and gentlemen, you have fifteen minutes." Jada set the timer at the front of the room. Those of you who are attorneys, get as much evidence as you need. I'll also need people to play the boys. You'll be on the witness stand so make sure you read up on each boy."

"I'll be Trevor!" Jada heard as she arranged the empty desks in the fashion of a courtroom. She wasn't sure who had claimed the main character, but she was more than excited to see how it would all play out.

■■■

"Ms. Harris, can you please quiet your class," Mrs. Glenn whispered, sticking her head into the door.

"Oh, sorry." Jada hushed her class before offering the woman an apologetic shrug. Inwardly, she wanted to laugh. It hadn't been the first time that the woman had stuck her head in the class. Jada had underestimated the students' devotion to their chosen roles. Even first period had embodied their characters with more tenacity than Jada could've possibly anticipated. Now that it was 7th period, Jada could finally breathe, knowing that her plan had actually been successful and would possibly encourage the students to read their homework assignments more often. The students who hadn't read found themselves overwhelmed by the activity; Even Adrian admitted that he would've performed better if he'd read the story the night before.

Now, Jada sat in the rolling chair behind her desk rubbing her sore feet. She hadn't sat down all day, yet another thing she hadn't considered when deciding to wear heels today. Suddenly, Principal Luther stuck his head in the door, tapping on it softly.

"Ms. Harris, you got a minute?" He shoved his hands in his pocket and walked towards her before she could answer.

"Ummm, sure." Jada lowered her feet and slid them

back into the heels.

"I heard you had a pretty interactive class today." He sat atop one of the desks, bunching his pants up as he got comfortable.

"Yeaaah, I'm sorry if you got any complaints about the noise. The students really got into it."

"Oh, no need to apologize." He waved off her comment. "These kids rarely get to act like kids. So, I think it's good for them." He rubbed his hands together before crossing his arms over his chest. "I came to speak with you about something different."

Jada wasn't sure what to expect. What could he possibly want from her? Rattling through possible scenarios, she assumed that he had come to ask her about bus or football duty, neither of which she really wanted to commit to, but she knew she'd have to do one of them.

"It seems that the advisor position for the Beta club hasn't been filled since the former advisor left." He stared at her pointedly. "Considering your knack with the students, I think it would be great if you became the new advisor. Is that something you would consider?"

Jada was surprised but elated. She'd much rather be the Beta club advisor than a chaperone for bus or football duty. "I actually wouldn't mind being the Beta club advisor, but only if I'm excused from football and bus duty."

He laughed jovially, clapping his hands together. "I think I can agree to that. I will let Ms. Allen know, and she will get all the paperwork for you." He stood and began to stroll towards the door. "Thanks for all you do, Ms. Harris."

"Thank you. I'll help you anyway I can." Jada said, standing and grabbing her tote.

He offered her a stiff nod before disappearing around the corner. Jada sat back in the chair, pleasantly surprised by their encounter. She had to admit that his behavior during the first faculty meeting had unsettled her a bit, but perhaps she had been entirely too quick to judge. Once again, Johnathan's words regarding judgment and giving people the benefit of the doubt seemed to deliver yet another swift kick to her ego.

After all, Principal Luther had entrusted the Beta club under her supervision; he couldn't be too bad of a leader. Could he?

Chapter Six

It had been five months since he had heard her voice, and he couldn't lie. He missed her like crazy. With her, it had been different. So many other women had accepted him for who he was, an ex-football player who had dropped out of college, smoked a pack of Newports a day, and lived paycheck-to-paycheck off temp jobs. Other women would have loved to simply take care of him because of his nice guy reputation, freshly manicured beard, and skills in the bedroom, but not Jada. Jada had been everything he never knew he wanted in a woman. She was independent, sassy, classy, super smart, and sexy. Everything about her screamed that she was out of his league, but he hadn't been able to stop himself from pursuing her ever since meeting her at the pharmacy years ago. When she had arrived for their first date wearing a pair of sweatpants, he had silently vowed to marry her. And when they had talked, it was as if she had read his mind word-for-word. She was so down-to-earth that he was actually taken aback, but her personality, the ways in which she maneuvered through life, determined, full of life, and laughter, had made him want to be around her almost every second of the day. And they had been that way. Her all over him, and he all over her. Until five months ago.

Caleb remembered the precise moment that she had given up on him. Ironically, that moment hadn't been the same day as their official break-up five months ago. It had happened two months prior when he had just started his new job at the Stockville Medical Clinic. While Jada was preparing to graduate from college and move back home to teach at Caldwin High, he was attempting to find steady income in hopes that he could give her a reason to stay with him. She had been overjoyed to learn about his new job, and he remembered the bright smile that spread across her face as he told her about his job duties and future promotion opportunities; her expressions made him smile. Suddenly, the smile had disappeared from his face, which Jada noticed instantly. She cuffed his arm as concerned lines disfigured her forehead.

"What's wrong, babe?" She asked.

"It's just that---," he murmured, "I don't want you thinking I'm weak if I ask you this."

She repositioned herself so that she was sitting directly in front of him, her dark eyes boring into his hazel brown ones. "Ask me what? Is this about me staying in Stockville?"

"Oh, no, no. I-I—," he sighed loudly. "I don't have the money to purchase my work uniform. I wondered if you would help me."

She released a sigh of relief. "That's it? I don't mind helping you. How much is the uniform?" She reached for her purse.

He held his hand out to stop her. "No, I don't want you giving me any money. I'd rather you come with me to the uniform store to buy it. That will make me feel better." He found it difficult to make eye contact with her. The very last thing he wanted to do was ask his lady for anything, especially to buy his work uniform.

Grabbing his chin and forcing his eyes to meet hers, Jada kissed him softly on the lips. "Babe, we're a team. You're making a step with this job, which isn't permanent, and you've just enrolled in school, so I'll ride this thing out with you to the end. I mean that." She kissed him again for further reassurance.

Caleb grabbed her hand and kissed the inside of her wrist softly before looking back up at her. "You know I appreciate you, right?"

"Uh uh, I don't know that at all," she taunted, rolling her eyes and pulling away from him.

He began to tickle her, sending her into a fit of laughter and conniption. "You still don't know?" He asked, threatening to continue his torture.

"I know! I know!" She yelled in between giggles. "Stop tickling me!" She slapped at his hands desperately.

Ceasing, he wrapped his arms around his waist, placing kisses in the nook of her neck. "I'm going to make you proud, babe, and then, I'm going to marry you and give you all our babies." He licked her ear lobe while tracing a trail with his fingertips from her forehead to her chin.

As promised, she'd purchased his uniform, never uttering a word of contempt or restlessness, and he'd been grateful. Things had been good. But then, she'd found out that he hadn't actually applied for re-entry into college. And like a stack of dominoes, the odds had fallen against him. On several occasions, he had managed to disappoint her. She'd found out that he hadn't quit smoking as promised, and his driver's license was suspended. It seemed that any small mistake warranted a rant or a question of their relationship, and the day she'd packed up her apartment, he'd seen the end in her eyes. She didn't say it, and she didn't have to because he knew it was coming. Five months ago, it had happened, and he found himself thinking about her every day. He arrived to work on time consistently; he went home and drank six or more beers every night. He had even started visiting the clinic's gym, anything to preoccupy his mind and erase her from his thoughts. It rarely worked, and even worse, he'd managed to gain weight.

Now, he was looking at a picture of her hugged up with some happy-go-lucky-looking guy on Facebook. He had to admit that when he first saw it, he had the mind to jump in his beat up Chevy and risk making the three hour trip to Michelin just to win her back, but his careful examination of the picture had stopped him in his tracks. Her smile said she was happy, but it didn't necessarily reach her eyes. He had seen this fake smile before, like when she had visited his mom's house for Thanksgiving dinner and had tried some of his mom's turkey and dressing. She had smiled after the first bite, but she never took a second bite. Her eyes had tipped Caleb off completely, and he'd chuckled to himself, just as he was doing now. There was no doubt that she liked the guy, but she wasn't totally invested just yet. And Caleb vowed to do whatever he could to keep it from ever happening.

Chapter Seven

"Delete." Jada muttered, her finger hovering hesitantly over the button. She stared at the picture, somehow surprised by how happy she looked. And then, she shifted her attention to the other person in the photo. A smiling Caleb stared back at her, his arms wrapped tightly around her, as they stood in her old apartment's kitchen. She remembered this moment as if it had just happened. She and Caleb had randomly decided to make Philly Cheesesteak sandwiches, so they'd driven to Wal-Mart at midnight just to grab loaves of French bread, onions, sirloin steaks, and Swiss cheese. They'd swatted at each other playfully from one aisle to another before finally rushing to the self-checkout station, arguing about who would pay, and driving back to her apartment with all the windows down and the wind blowing through her hair. They'd cooked and bragged about their skills and laughed at themselves for being so easily impressed with each other. Then, they had watched *Megamind*, well, the movie had watched them canoodle and whisper in each other's ears non-stop.

Now, looking at the picture pitched Jada into a realm of nostalgia that made her slightly uncomfortable. She truly liked Johnathan, but lately, she'd found herself wondering, *what if*. What if she had waited a bit longer for Caleb? What if she had simply tried to understand why Caleb lied to her about school and smoking? What if she hadn't met Johnathan? She quickly pressed the button and the picture instantly disappeared from her timeline. She found herself fighting an urge to cry, which wasn't new. Every time she deleted one of their pictures, it seemed to solidify the end. She would be lying if she said that she had wanted the relationship to end because she didn't. She had spent years trying to avoid the inevitable end.

Caleb had a heart and genuineness about him that she had been looking for, and once she'd gotten it, it just didn't seem to be enough. And she couldn't help but think about how different and alike he and Johnathan were. They were both good with their hands but on different levels. Johnathan was an artist while Caleb could fix any plumbing, electrical, or construction problem. They were both extremely likable and friendly, always giving people the benefit of the doubt. However, Johnathan was far more ambitious and adventurous, whereas Caleb was more attentive and devilishly rugged, which Jada liked.

Suddenly, Jada's phone vibrated in her lap, and she welcomed the distraction. Flipping her phone over, she looked down to see Caleb's face smiling back at her. She had never deleted his contact picture from her SIM card, and here he was calling her. The time couldn't be worse. She flipped the phone back onto its face while wringing her fingers in her lap. The phone continued to vibrate.

"Don't answer it, J," she whispered, standing quickly and sending her phone falling to the carpeted floor. She walked to the kitchen swiftly, grabbing some grapes, rinsing them gently, and placing them in a bowl. "What could he possibly want?" she asked, shaking her head as she realized she was talking aloud to herself. Shuffling to her bedroom, she plopped a handful of grapes in her mouth and swept the phone from the floor. As if on cue, the phone began to vibrate again, and Caleb's face stared back at her.

Before she could think about it, she swiped right, answering his call. She didn't say anything because she didn't trust herself.

"Jada?" His voice sounded breathy, full of anticipation. He seemed to have been holding his breath just as she had been holding hers.

"Yeah?" she asked quietly, sitting the bowl on her nightstand and sliding to the floor, her knees positioned under her chin.

"I- I didn't expect you to answer." He sighed heavily.

"How are you?"

"I-I'm doing fine." She folded her legs beneath her, leaning back casually against her bed. "I didn't expect to hear from you, Caleb. It's been a minute." She slapped her forehead, not sure why she'd said that.

"Yeah, I know. I thought we both needed space after the—um, you know—separation." He chuckled nervously.

"Right. How have you been?" She asked, attempting to sound nonchalant and unconcerned. But she was hanging on to every word. She could hardly breathe out of fear that she'd miss something.

"Well—um, I've been good. Just working and stuff. Nothing major."

"Yeah, I understand. Me too." She laughed.

There was a long silence, and for Jada, it seemed that they were conversing without any words. Neither of them knew what to say; yet, they had so much to say to each other. Even more, they were glad just to hear each other's voice, at least that's what Jada felt.

"I just like knowing you're on the other end of this phone, Jada. I really miss you," he said softly.

Jada flinched, looking about her room. It was as if he had been there or inside of her head, reading her thoughts. Something inside of her seemed to leap, spreading throughout her body and emitting satisfaction that she didn't know she'd needed before his call. Stuttering, she said, "I-I miss you, too, Caleb, but my decision hasn't changed."

"I know. I know. You told me to get myself together and then come find you, and I'm willing to do that." He cleared his throat, which was thick with emotion. "But Jada, don't fall in love with the new dude. I'm coming back for you, and I will marry you, even if it means breaking his heart. My feelings for you haven't changed, and they never will." The line went silent.

Jada pulled the phone away from her ear and stared at it. She didn't know how long she'd been sitting there until the phone began to vibrate in her hand, and Johnathan's face popped up on the screen. She groaned aloud and tossed it on the bed behind her. She couldn't possibly speak to him right now. She knew that her voice would betray her.

Standing, she grabbed the bowl of grapes and strolled into the small kitchen space, dumping the grapes into the trash and startling her cat Duchess out of her sleep. The cat meowed out of annoyance and curled back up on the sofa. She shook her head as she thought about Johnathan. He was perfect. So, why was she questioning their relationship now? She was afraid of her own answer and even more frightened that she felt like she was cheating. But on whom?

Chapter Eight

Today was the day, the Beta club's first official event, and Jada had to admit that she was more excited than the students. She had fallen into her new role as the club's advisor so easily. Even when they had held the first meeting and she had made her vision for the club clear, the students seemed optimistic about it. They had freely thrown out ideas and suggestions during the first meeting, which adjourned with the entire group deciding to induct new members first, then hold a school-wide bake sale followed by a lavish but reasonable Breast Cancer Awareness program. Tonight, they would be holding the induction ceremony, welcoming nineteen students into the club. Looking around at the black, gold, and white balloons, the carefully decorated cake, and all of the current members dressed in white shirts and black bottoms, she felt that she'd fully transitioned into the Caldwin High family. On more than one occasion, the students had told her that they were used to adults in the school failing to follow through on their word. But looking at their faces right now, she could see that they believed in her, and she didn't intend to let them down.

"It looks pretty good, huh, Ms. H?" Randy, a tall, lanky boy asked, coming to stand beside her.

Jada smiled up at him and looked at the fountain that was daintily spewing juice for guests. "Yeah, you all did very well."

"Awww, we only did what you told us to do. By the way, that little fountain thing is super cool." He smiled back at her goofily before sauntering off to his group of friends, who were taking pictures in front of the fountain.

"This is probably the best set-up I've seen since being here," the librarian, Ms. Watkins, whispered, coming around her desk to stand beside Jada.

"Thanks, Ms. Watkins. I'm just trying to do what I can with what I have. These are great kids."

"Yeah, they are. And you—You're a great teacher, Ms. Harris. Half these teachers never even bring the students to the library. You had the freshman in here before I knew it. Even I felt the pressure because I finally had to work," she chuckled. "Don't let anyone tell you that you're not a good teacher, and I do mean *anyone*." She gave Jada a pointed glance before walking back behind her large desk.

Jada spotted her mom and two sisters walking in the door, carrying armfuls of paper plates. A large smile spread across Jada's face. No matter what, they would always support her, even when it meant bringing plates that one of the students forgot.

"You've done a great job with this, Ms. Harris," Principal Luther said, sliding beside her and startling her. "The kids look happy."

Jada looked up at him with a smirk. "Thank you, Mr.

Luther."

"Not a problem." He pulled his keys out of his pocket and began to wrestle one of them off the loop. "Look, I'm not going to be able to stay very long. Do you think you can lock up the school when you all are finished?" He extended the key to her.

Gawking, Jada stared at the key. "I—um—I have never locked up the school, Mr. Luther. I'm not sure that I feel comfortable doing that."

"Ms. Harris, I'm not asking you to find Osama Bin Laden, just to lock up the front doors. I will make sure that the other doors are secured before I leave. Can you do that for me?"

"Um—okay. Am I the only faculty member here?"

"As far as I know. You got this." He placed the key on the desktop behind them before strutting to sit in a chair positioned close to the door.

Jada wasn't sure what to make of his request. It seemed fairly simple, but for Jada it was just another responsibility he had placed in her lap at the last minute. She knew she was probably making too much of it, but it meant that she had to clear the building, ensure that all of the lights were turned off, and of course, lock the door. Maybe she was making too much of it, but she would have felt better knowing that there was an administrator in the facility. Luckily, her mom and sisters were in attendance, so she had help if she needed it. *Thank you, God, for my family*, she prayed silently.

"Ladies and Gentlemen, please take your seats as we commence with the induction program," the club president requested confidently.

Jada smiled as she watched Destiny summon everyone's attention. Her nerves had calmed, and she commanded the room with such grace and strength that Jada nearly forgot about her breakdown earlier in the day. Jada had consoled her, assuring her that she was more than prepared for the task and reminding her why she had been selected to be the president in the first place. Looking at her now, she was elegantly poised, her words flowing smoothly as she made eye contact with the audience, just as she and Jada had practiced.

"Now, I ask that all inductees please grab the candlestick under your chair and stand," she instructed. Cameras flashed as the students lit their candles, passing the flame to their neighbors, and then repeating the Beta club pledge as stated by Destiny. Jada looked on in amazement. Everything had occurred as planned. And even as the ceremony ended, she watched as parents mingled and enjoyed cake with their scholars, stopping ever-so-often to snap a quick picture.

"I remember doing this with you and your siblings," her mom whispered, sneaking up beside her.

Jada smiled and placed her arm on her mother's shoulder, pulling her in for a hug. "Yeah, can you believe that now I'm over the club?"

"I sure can!" Her mom exclaimed. "You were always into something and if you think about it, you were always encouraging and teaching your siblings. It makes total sense to me." She hugged Jada back, placing a soft kiss on her cheek.

"Thanks for coming, Ma. You don't know how good it feels to see you all coming through the door." Jada squeezed her tighter.

"Yes, I do. That's why I come," she winked at Jada. "Now, let's get this place cleaned up so we can blow this popsicle stand."

Jada chuckled and proceeded to assign duties to each group of students. The students accepted their assignments willingly, tackling their tasks with diligence. In less than thirty minutes, Jada turned off the lights in the library and walked to the front door, her mother and sisters in tow. She smiled as she turned the key in the lock. It was still her first year of teaching, and here she was securing the school building. Maybe *she* should look into being a school principal in the future, after all. If Ms. Calloway could do it, surly she could. And actually be good at it.

"Ms. Harris, can you come to Mr. Luther's office during your planning period?" Ms. Allen's voice spoke calmly from the speaker box.

"Yes, ma'am," Jada responded, not sure why she was being summoned.

The bell sounded, and the students sauntered out of the classroom, dropping their assignments in the black tray on their way out. Jada waited patiently as the last student filed out of the room before closing and locking the door. Walking to the office, she considered all of the possibilities. She had made sure the door was locked after last night's induction ceremony. She hadn't been late, and she had attended both faculty meetings last month. Nothing came to mind.

"How you doin', Ms. Harris?" Ms. Allen asked, beaming at Jada.

Jada smiled back. "I can't complain. How are you?"

"Girl, other than having to deal with y'all's headache of a principal, I'm just fine." The woman swatted the air dramatically.

Jada chuckled. She and Ms. Allen had definitely come a long way, especially considering their very first encounter. Jada would even say that Ms. Allen liked her a little, at least enough to keep her up on the school's gossip.

"Headache?" Jada frowned, as she signed the visitation list, a new practice that had been implemented since the removal of the former principals. It made her feel dirty, even though she hadn't been implicated. "What did he do this time, Ms. Allen?"

Ms. Allen rolled her eyes, signing her name besides Jada's neat signature. "What don't he do? He's always asking me questions, as if I'm the principal, or something. I'm telling you, he may have a doctorate degree, but that man should not have come out of retirement. He doesn't know what he's doing here," she whispered.

"Maybe you're being too hard on him, Ms. Allen.

He's out of practice." Jada pulled the heavy glass door open, as Ms. Allen walked towards her.

"No, baby, I've been here long enough to know out-of-practice and boo-boo-the-fool. He don't know what he's doin'." She dropped the clipboard on the counter matter-of-factly and plopped down in her rolling chair, before tucking her skirt between her legs and announcing Jada's arrival through the phone.

Jada waited, fidgeting with her thumbs by her side. The layers of security just to see a member of administration always made her nervous.

"Yes, sir, she signed in," Ms. Allen drawled into the receiver. "Yes, sir, I signed the sheet, too." She looked at Jada and pointed to the receiver in annoyance. "Yes, sir, I put the time of entrance. Can I send her in?" She spoke through gritted teeth, rolling her eyes and scribbling on a small piece of paper. Finally, she hung up the phone and spun around to Jada. "You see what I'm saying? He focuses on the smallest things, but I think it's to hide the fact that he can't do the bigger things." She sighed heavily. "Anyway, he's ready for you."

Jada nodded stiffly before walking down the short hallway. She knocked on the open door before stepping across the threshold.

Mr. Luther swiveled away from the computer and motioned for her to have a seat across from his desk. "Hi, Ms. Harris. Just give me one minute to make a few notes."

"Sure," she said, glancing around the office. The walls had been painted a smoldering red with gray and black stripes in various places. Plaques that echoed his accomplishments in different schools lined the walls, and a framed photograph of he and his wife sat snuggly in the corner of his desk. Compared to the last principal, his office was quite simple. There weren't any fraternity portraits or student notes. Other than the one picture, there were no personal touches, nothing that connected him to Caldwin High on a personal level.

"I know you're probably wondering why I called you

here." He leaned back in his chair, interlocking his fingers under his chin. "It has been brought to my attention that your classes are extremely loud."

Jada blinked slowly, hoping she had misheard him. "I-I'm sorry. What?" She leaned forward in the uncomfortably hard chair.

"Well, I have received complaints about your classroom being too noisy." He pulled a sheet of paper from a manila folder.

"You called me here, during my planning period, for that? We had already discussed this." Jada scoffed. "I thought you understood."

"We discussed it very briefly. It may not be very important to you, but it's extremely important for the teachers and students around you. I hope that you will be more mindful in the future."

"No, I think I can say that my classes are very lively, and at times, the students can get loud. All of our classes get loud from time-to-time. I just wished you had advised the teachers or whomever to speak with me about it first. This hardly calls for a sit-down in the principal's office. Wouldn't you agree?"

"No, I think they brought it to me because it's my job. But going forward, I'm sure we won't have this conversation again, right?" He stared at her pointedly, pushing a sheet of paper toward her.

"Well, Mr. Luther, I'm not a child. So, there's no need to speak to me as if I am one." She grabbed the paper. "And what is this?" Her eyes ran over the document labeled Behavioral Reprimand.

"That's the new form we're using whenever we discuss particular matters with teachers and staff. It's just a warning sheet. You just have to sign showing that we talked, that you understand the expectations that were communicated to you, and that you intend to abide by them. It's just a little paper trail." He peeked at her over his glasses, his bald head gleaming.

Jada chuckled inwardly before pushing the sheet back

toward him. "I'm not signing that."

"You have to. It's not an official write up or anything. It's just for documentation purposes." He slowly removed his glasses and wiped them down with a Kleenex.

"I don't have to sign anything. However, I will write my disagreement with this whole thing on there." She grabbed the paper and simply wrote, *I, Jada Harris, do not agree with this document or the means by which I was summoned to Mr. Judge Luther's office on today.* She dated the form and pushed it back towards him.

He snatched it up and placed it back in the folder. "Fine, Ms. Harris. But understand this—" He replaced his glasses back on the tip of his nose. "If you want to move up in any school, you have to be open for criticism and willing to accept change, no matter how small it may seem to you."

"I'm afraid that you have misread this situation. I am not defiant because of the complaints, but the manner in which you handled it is all wrong. Couldn't I reprimand you for leaving me with the key to the school building last night?

For pressing me to complete a task that is expected of *you*? For allowing me to be the only faculty or staff member in the school?" She watched him shift uncomfortably in his seat. She knew she had definitely hit a nerve. "See, Mr. Luther, you, too, must be open for criticism and, also, *know* the school's policies. You have yet to provide the basic professional needs for several teachers, yet, here you are making time to reprimand *me*." She stood and smoothed out her skirt before walking to the door and closing it behind her.

"See," Ms. Allen hissed, her arms folded loosely across her chest. "He's backwards as heck." She shook her head and turned back to her computer.

Jada opened the main office door, finally breathing when she entered the lunchroom. The sound of heels clicking caught her attention, and she came face-to-face with a smiling Ms. Calloway.

"I sure hope that you can better control your students." The woman drawled, walking past Jada. "I would hate for you to get a full write-up next time."

Jada knew it. Mr. Luther hadn't received multiple complaints, just one. One that had more than likely suggested that he call her into the office. Now, Jada realized that the reprimand form had Ms. Calloway's work written all over it. It had been her doing, and it only proved that she had somehow gotten Mr. Luther on her side.

"You know, Ms. Calloway, I feel sorry for you. You couldn't advance through your talent so you had to resort to using your family ties and low-handed antics, tearing other people down, even if it's another Black woman. You are pathetic, and you won't win."

The woman turned, a dark grin spread across her face, as her honey brown eyes glistened with hate. "Honey, don't you see. The assistant superintendent is my brother. I'm now assistant principal. Plus, I have the principal eating out of my hands because he has no idea what he's doing. I'm already winning." She pursed her lips and strolled away, glancing back at Jada in victory as she rounded the corner.

Chapter Nine

"I mean, babe, *are* your classes too loud?" Johnathan asked quietly after listening to Jada rant on and on about the meeting.

Jada rolled her eyes and pulled the phone away from her ear, staring at it with disgust. She had hoped that Johnathan would finally pick up on her mood and know that she didn't always need him siding with the opposition. It was really starting to get on her nerves. He always made it seem as though she was being a big baby about everything.

"Hello?" His voice was beginning to annoy her. "Jada, are you there, baby?"

"Um, yeah, I'm here." She forced out a yawn. "Look,

I'm really tired, so I think I'm going to turn in for the night."

"Um, Jada, baby, it's the weekend. I really wanna talk to you," he pouted.

Now who's being the baby, she thought, throwing the peanut butter and jelly sandwich she'd made into the garbage. She'd suddenly lost her appetite. She hated that his voice didn't give her chills like it used to. And she knew that he was intentionally using his sexy, sad voice, but it wasn't doing anything for her right now. More than anything, she just wanted to be left alone.

"Yeah, I know. I'm just so tired." She sighed loudly.

There was silence. "Okay, babe, I'll let you go." He drawled. "I love you."

"Love you, too." She quickly ended the call and walked out onto her patio. Mid-September always brought the fondest breeze. She watched a lone, dark orangish leaf float down onto the patio, joining the other fallen leaves. Jada inhaled slowly. Somehow, the air smelled of pine and hot chocolate, and she loved it. Being that the Fall was her favorite season, she was always anticipating its arrival. Looking around at the naturally-hued stones that her landscaper had just installed, she was pleased. She could finally put her backyard to use. She sank into the swinging hammock, knowing she'd found the perfect resting spot.

The sound of her phone ringing interrupted her thoughts. She frowned, struggled to untie herself from the ropes, and jogged back into the house, snatching her phone up off the countertop. It was her mother.

"Hey, Ma. What's goi—"

"Jada," her mom cut her off. "Caleb's here."

Jada found herself inhaling slowly again, but her heart was pounding quickly. "Caleb? Um, what?" She ran her trembling hand through her hair.

"He came looking for you." Her mom sounded much calmer than Jada would have expected.

"Okay, I'm on my way."

■■

Pulling into her mother's driveway, Jada's mind

seemed to be stuck in space, floating from place to place, out of her realm of control. She switched the engine off and stared at the shiny, black Chevy Impala parked beside the mailbox. It had to be Caleb's, and it was definitely an upgrade from the beat-up car he'd received from his mother. Jada wondered what it meant, all of it. His phone call. Him and his car. Him showing up to her mom's house unannounced. Was he really coming back for her?

She yanked down the visor mirror, applying a thin layer of pink lip-gloss onto her full lips. Luckily, her curls had still been intact despite the long, humid day they'd been through. She scrunched a few curls in her hand, hoping to give them just a bit more volume. It didn't work. She wrapped a lone curl around her finger, hoping it would help. The curl returned to its lanky spiral. Frustrated, she snapped the visor closed. *Jada, girl, what are you doing?* She thought, shaking her head and placing both hands on the steering wheel. *This is no big deal. He's the same Caleb as before.* She fumbled around in her purse for a stick of gum, finding it at the very bottom. Pulling it out, she noticed a small flash of light emitting from it. She held the slender aluminum packet in front of her face, as the abandoned ring slid down and rested against her finger. Caleb had promised to replace it with a real engagement ring as soon as he got on his feet, but she'd thrown it in her purse on the night of their break-up. She stared at it in disbelief. It was ironic that it would decide to make an appearance on today out of all days.

Movement out of the corner of her eye caught her attention. She watched in pure amazement as a clean-shaven and handsomely dressed Caleb rounded the corner, stuffing his hands in the pockets of his suit pants, a devilish and shy grin spread across his face. Jada froze, her mouth dry and eyes taking it all in. The fine hairs on his jawline were crisply shaped and combed, framing his face in that rugged appeal that Jada had seen when she'd first met him. Jada had never seen him in a suit, but now, she knew why. He threatened every vow she'd made to God. The Navy, blue pants and blazer were tailored to every muscle, the white-collar shirt showing off a small patch of hair on his chest. He wore a thin, gold chain tastefully draped about his neck. She couldn't help but feel underdressed in the presence of Mr. GQ himself. He continued to walk towards her, his smile never leaving; his eyes softening more and more with each step towards her.

Finally, he was standing by her car door. Jada didn't miss the hint of moisture in the corner of his eyes, encouraging her own emotions to come to the forefront.

Hello, he mouthed, staring back at her with intensity, as if asking her for permission.

Not sure what she was agreeing to, Jada nodded stiffly, a tear escaping from her eye.

As if on cue, he slowly pulled her car door open, reached down for her hand, and gently pulled her up until her eyes were meeting his. He kissed her hand softly, before cupping it in his large hands.

"I've missed you, Jada." He wrapped one of her curls around his finger. "I came back for you, like I said I would."

Jada swallowed hard. "C-Caleb, what are you doing?" She dragged her eyes away from his, looking down at the cobblestone driveway.

He pulled her chin up so that her eyes stared back into his and wiped away a tear traveling down her face. "I told you that when it comes to me and you, it may be bigger than me. It may be bigger than you. But absolutely nothing is bigger than you and me. And baby," he pulled both of her hands up to his shoulders. "I meant that. I love you too much to ever lose you. If you will have me, I want to spend the rest of my life proving that to you."

Jada couldn't help the tears that streamed down her face. She smiled up at him, grabbing his face with both hands, and pulling it down until his lips were mere inches from hers. "I love you, Caleb Moore," she whispered.

He captured her lips in a searing and hungry kiss, his arms circling her waist and pulling her in tightly against his hard frame. Jada stood on her tiptoes, meeting each of his kisses with desperate kisses of her own. She could feel every inch of him pressing into her body, and even though she knew her family might be watching, she couldn't seem to pull herself away from him. Jada could feel wetness on her face, as the stubble from his beard rubbed against her cheek. She didn't know if the tears came from her or him, but right now, she didn't care. She didn't care that he had a new car, or a career. She just needed this moment of pure happiness and sameness, familiarity.

Pulling away abruptly, Caleb looked down at her, removing a small box from his pocket.

Jada gasped, "Caleb, w-wait—." She attempted to block the contents of the box from her view. "We don't have—." The box popped open. Jada stared down into the box in confusion. There was nothing there.

Chuckling, Caleb pulled a folded sheet of paper from the slit of the box. "I know, I know. We're not all the way ready for that step, but I didn't want to come here empty handed, with nothing to show for myself." He clumsily unfolded the paper, dropping the box in the progress. They both laughed at his inability to ever complete a task smoothly. It unnerved Jada that she had even missed his imperfections. Unlike Johnathan----*Oh, crap, Johnathan!* She thought, biting her bottom lip nervously.

Sensing her sudden mood swing, Caleb laced his fingers through hers, forcing her eyes back to his face. "Whoa, look, should I have proposed?" The frown lines etched in his forehead matched his concerned expression. "I really didn't think you would have me back so soon, so I took it—." He bent his knees to get a better view of her face. His eyes were filled with questions and worry.

Jada shook her head vigorously. "No, I just—wait— the box. You bought a ring?" She starred back at him with anticipation. Her hands began to perspire in his.

He lowered his eyes sheepishly. "Y-yeah, I did. The first thing I bought with my first check from my new job was a newer car and this suit." He extended his arms and looked down at his trousers, before pulling Jada back close. "With the second check, I purchased the ring I'd use to ask for your hand in marriage."

Jada couldn't breathe. It was all too much. A ring? She loosened her hands from his and stepped back until her back was touching the driver side door of her car. She passed her hands over her face in frustration. "Wait, new job?" She crossed her arms over chest, her forehead riddled with wrinkles. "You had just started a new job when we broke up? And why did you buy a ring? I don't understand."

He stepped closer to her. "That's why I have this." He waved the piece of paper in front of her.

Jada held up her hands to stop his approach. "What's on the paper?"

He extended the paper to her. "I think it would be best if you read all the changes I've made since our, um, break-up."

Jada slowly reached for the worn piece of paper. She read the first line, her head lifting quickly to stare Caleb down. "Did you really quit smoking this time? Or?"

He held up both hands, then patted down his pockets.

"Yeah. It's been hard, but I'm really trying. You can smell my car."

Partially satisfied, Jada read the next two lines. "You work at the bank now? What about the hospital and your new dream of being an emergency technician? And what do you mean by school?" She tried not to sound as anxious with her questions, but despite her musing, she couldn't help herself.

"I still wanna be an emergency technician, but my job at the hospital wasn't gonna give me enough income to live and go to school. So, I picked up a part-time job at Wyndell Bank in Stockville. And I enrolled in night classes at the community college so that I could work towards my goal to be an emergency tech. I start classes next week. It'll take me a year." He smirked back at her.

Jada exhaled slowly, refolding the paper. "Wow, Caleb. I'm really happy for you. It seems that you have been doing just fine without me." She pushed her curls behind her ears, wondering why she felt even more emotional now than before.

Caleb used the opportunity to step closer to her.

"Jada," he whispered. "I'm doing better because of you. I've spent the past few years living in the past. All I knew in high school was football, so when I got injured, I didn't know what else to do. I really felt like I couldn't do anything else. I was in a relationship for years with a woman who never motivated or encouraged me. My parents didn't even push me. As long as I had a steady job, they didn't have much to say." He reached for hands. "But fast forward a few years, and here you come, waltzing into my life and telling me all these things I never thought I could be. You see me in a better light than I see myself. Your ambition scares me sometimes. Look at you. In the four years that I have known you, you've accomplished every single goal on your list. I guess, I'm so afraid to disappoint you that I don't try, but my life seems to stop running smoothly when you're not in it." He pulled her hair from behind her ears, staring in her eyes. "I can live without you, but, woman, I don't even wanna try. You're my wife, Jada. There is no doubt in my mind that

God made you just for me."

"But—" He cut her words off with a quick kiss that seemed to last forever. "Caleb, I'm in—" He silenced her with another kiss, his hands framing her face as his tongue teased hers. He slowly ended the kiss, lightly nipping at her bottom lip with his teeth.

"I don't want to hear anything but a yes. Yes, you'll go out with me tonight. I've made plans." His eyes twinkled as he smiled down at her.

Jada felt her defenses melting. *What the heck?*, she thought. *One night never hurt anyone.* She grinned up at him. "So, you just knew I'd say yes, huh?" She asked, swatting at his chest.

He grabbed her hand. "No, you always said that you should let a person tell you no. Don't tell yourself no." He gently ushered her towards the passenger side of his car. "Wishful thinking," he chuckled, opening the door and helping her inside before closing the door and running to the other side. Just then, Jada's phone sounded.

It was a text from Johnathan: *I know you're probably sleeping, but I miss you like crazy. I realize that I didn't really hear you out earlier, and I'm sorry. Call me as soon as you wake up. :)*

Jada's breathe caught in her throat, throwing her into a coughing fit. She struggled to find air.

"Baby, you good?" Caleb asked, sliding into the driver seat and patting her back lightly.

"What?" Jada cleared her throat loudly. "Yeah, yeah. I'm good. I'm good." She accepted a bottle of water he'd pulled from his backseat. She couldn't untwist the cap fast enough; she threw the liquid down her throat, hoping it would drown the mess she'd gotten herself into. Sensing Caleb's concern, she threw him a reassuring smile that didn't quite reach her eyes. She quickly looked out the window, hoping to avoid his prying gaze.

He laced his fingers through hers while putting the car into gear and pulling away from the curb, just as Jada saw her mother's blinds snap closed.

Chapter Ten

Ding-dong! Jada woke suddenly. The sound was invasive, piercing. The bright sun bore into her barely open eyes, and she groaned while struggling to roll over to the other side of the bed, frowning when she saw Caleb's shirtless form stumbling from one side of the bed to the hall. They had only fallen asleep four hours ago after spending most of the night talking and exchanging heavy kisses.

"I'll get it," he grumbled, his bare feet slapping against the hardwood floor. Jada slid up until her back rested against the headboard and rubbed the crust out of her eyes. She thought about their date. It was the first time that Caleb had actually planned a date for them. They'd had dinner at the Chop's Lobster Bar before viewing a play at the Hattiloo Theatre. As he'd glided down the streets of Memphis, Caleb had rested his hand on her thigh and squeezed it lightly while grinning at her. Later, he'd taken her to the Cheesecake Factory where he'd still managed to be his clumsy self, knocking his drink over when he'd fed her a piece of his cheesecake. He had been mortified, but Jada's giggles had made him laugh. They had agreed that the date had been nice, but they both just wanted a McChicken from McDonald's. The night had ended with Jada inviting him in, and now someone was ringing the doorbell incessantly.

She heard him disarm the alarm, not sure when she had given him the code. The door beeped as he opened it. But there were no words.

"Jada!" Caleb yelled. "You might want to come to the door."

Concerned and confused, she crawled out of the bed. After fishing through her dresser for a t-shirt, she pulled it over her tank top, peeked at the large floor mirror, and ran her fingers through her hair, licking her finger to wipe some white residue from her cheek. Resolute, she walked out of her bedroom and towards the door. Caleb's chiseled form blocked her view of the person standing on the other side of the door. Upon hearing her approach, he looked back at her with a flat expression before stepping aside. Jada stood frozen in the middle of the hall, as she took in the figure. Johnathan was glaring at Caleb. His heated stare transferred to Jada as he assessed her from head to toe. His jaw began to flex with anger. Jada inhaled sharply.

Caleb cleared his throat before walking towards her, stopping by her side. "Look, I popped up on you yesterday. So, handle your business and just let me know. But know this, I'm gonna keep coming until we're together." He kissed her forehead and squeezed her arms before padding back into her bedroom, sloppily throwing on his shirt, and strutting past a fuming Johnathan. Jada watched as his car slowly pulled out of her driveway.

"Are you going to invite me in?" Johnathan asked

sarcastically, brushing past Jada as she opened the door
wider. Any hope Jada had that this might be a pleasant
conversation flew out of the window. She closed the door
and quietly followed him into the living room, where he
threw his bag onto the floor and turned to her, his hand
cupping his chin. "So, when were you gonna tell me about
him, Jada?" He spoke very calmly, but his eyes were
shooting daggers at her.

"Johnathan," she whispered, sitting on the arm of her
loveseat. "He just popped up at my mom's house last night. I
didn't—"

He looked at her, his head cocked to one side. "Last
night? You mean last night when you told me you were
going to sleep? That last night?" He crossed his arms over his
chest, his eyes bulging with anticipation.

"Are you gonna listen or just grill me?" Jada snapped,
crossing her legs at the ankle. She noticed him biting his
lower lip and figured it would be best to use a softer
approach. After all, she understood why he was mad. She

couldn't say that she would even be this calm if he'd put her in this same predicament. "Look, I want to be as open with you as possible. Will you sit down so that we can really talk?" She attempted a small smile, waving towards the armchair behind him. She read the hesitation on his face. "Johnathan, please."

Exhaling in resignation, he slid into the chair, but he still looked at her expectantly. "I'm sitting and listening." He leaned forward, resting his elbows on his knees.

Jada straightened her back and spoke softly. "My mom called me when I got off the phone with you last night and told me that Caleb had just popped up at her house because he didn't know where I lived. So, I went over there; we talked. He took me on a date. By the time that the date was over, it was late so I told him he could stay here. That's all." She linked her fingers together in her lap, fidgeting nervously.

Johnathan seemed to soften a bit, but then, he looked at her pointedly. "And *nothing* happened between you?"

Jada shook her head. "No, nothing like *that* happened."

"But you did kiss him, right?" He looked back at her with that knowing smile, that one that told her that he was only asking for confirmation.

She looked away in embarrassment, rubbing her hands down her legs. All of a sudden her hands felt clammy and sweaty. She didn't know where to put them.

"Right," he scoffed. He snatched his bag up from the floor and stood abruptly.

"Johnathan, where are you going?" She asked, looking up at him. "I told you the truth."

He chuckled inwardly, placing the bag on his shoulder. "What am I supposed to say, Jada? Thank you?" He waved her off and walked towards the door.

Jada jumped from the couch, walking swiftly behind him. "No, I don't want a thank you, Johnathan. I just want you to understand. I didn't ask him to pop up last night. I had no idea."

He turned towards her suddenly. "No!" he yelled. "You don't get to play the victim here. You *chose* to go on a date with him. You *chose t*o sleep in the same bed with him. You *chose* to put what we got goin' on in jeopardy. This didn't just happen to you, Jada. The problem is that you don't know what you want. And my problem is that I asked you where you stood in the beginning!" He was standing mere inches from her now. Jada had never seen him so passionate about anything other than art. But there was no way that she would let him try to blame all of this on her and pretend that they hadn't discussed this beforehand.

"That's not fair. I told you where I stood!" She placed her hands on her hips. "I told you that I had just gotten out of a four-year relationship with him. And we agreed to go my speed, and I've been going with the flow on everything, everything. I didn't know he was coming last night, and I didn't know you were coming today. So, excuse me if I haven't sorted out my thoughts just yet! I will show you out!" She yelled, walking past him and yanking open the door. Her eyes remained fastened to the floor. She didn't trust herself to keep the tears in much longer.

He walked towards her slowly. "You know, coming here, I just wanted to be next to you and to apologize for not listening to you and giving you the support that you need. But now I see why you dislike my advice. You only consider your own feelings, no one else's. I get that he popped up on you, but for you to place your own confusion above what I feel right now is not what I signed up for." He shuffled out of the door and down the driveway to his rental car.

Jada closed the door and pressed her back against it. In all her life, she had never found herself in a love triangle, and she definitely didn't like the nauseous feeling resting in her stomach. She needed to find a solution quick, but how could she get her heart and her mind on the same page?

Chapter Eleven

A long black and white blazer and a pair of freshly-creased white, wide-leg pants. Nude wedge heels. Mauve lipstick. Jada twirled in the mirror, enjoying the power exuding from her. When she'd ventured to her closet this morning, she'd been looking for something that said, *Don't mess with me*. And her eyes had landed on the tailored suit she'd bought over the summer. Pulling it out, she'd grinned, sure that it would give her the feeling she was aiming for. Although she didn't feel in control of her personal life at the moment, she couldn't afford to dwell on it now. When she'd left Caldwin High last Friday, she'd finally felt like the reigns were in her hands. Within the first month, Principal

Luther had made her the Beta Club advisor, ACT prep instructor, and a Senior class sponsor. She hadn't said it then, but it felt that he had dropped multiple weights on her shoulder; however, she'd taken them in stride. But last Friday when he'd attempted to write her up, she had felt inclined to speak her mind, and no matter what Johnathan said, it was necessary. Mr. Luther couldn't heavily rely on her and unfairly discipline her in the same breath. She wasn't going to stand for it and allow him to meddle with her, even if Ms. Calloway was the brains behind the operation.

She flipped her hair over her shoulder and winked at the fierce diva that stared back at her in the mirror. Just then, her cat Duchess strolled into the bathroom, wrapping herself around Jada's ankle. Jada bent down to stroke her, chuckling at the small purr that ran through her body. "Duch, mama is getting herself together. Don't worry." The cat looked up at her and walked away, as if bored with Jada. Jada giggled, glad that out of everyone Duchess had remained her feisty self. Jada grabbed her purse off the armchair and opened the front door, making sure to activate the alarm. Just as she stepped onto her porch, a blur of fur darted past her and out of the house. "Duchess!" Jada yelled, panicked. Walking out to her driveway, Jada looked around. The cat was nowhere in sight. Jada bent to look under her car, knowing that was usually the cat's hiding spot, but she wasn't there. "Duchess, please, I have to get to work," Jada whispered, glancing down at her watch.

■■■

With her natural tresses disheveled and slightly puffy from humidity and perspiration, Jada half-jogged, half-marched into the front office to sign in. The first period tardy bell had rang less than ten minutes ago, and she knew the rest of her day wouldn't run very smoothly.

"Sorry. Sorry," she said breathlessly, hoping to calm the look of disappointment on Ms. Allen's face. It didn't work. The woman grabbed the clipboard from Jada and proceeded to highlight Jada's name, as she'd been instructed. Even if she wanted to give Jada a pass this time, she couldn't because Principal Luther was already aware and ranting about her tardiness.

"Tsk. Tsk," the woman said, eyeing Jada. "Ms. Calloway is in your class now. Why are you late?" She put both hands on her hips.

Jada rolled her eyes. Ms. Calloway was the very last person she needed to see this morning. She readjusted her tote strap on her shoulder. "My cat ran out of the house, and it took me forever to find her."

Ms. Allen's expression softened. "Oh, I'm glad you found her, but you know the principal and that Ms. Calloway are gunnin' for you. I don't know what happened between you two last Friday, but he made a beeline for your classroom this morning. When he didn't find you there for the first bell, he went on a rampage in here." She plopped back into her chair, readjusting the hot pink glasses on her face. "Just want you to be on the lookout."

"Thanks, Ms. Allen. I appreciate the warning." She attempted to blindly fix her hair and strolled out of the office, aiming to look more unbothered than she actually felt. Rounding the corner towards her hall, she ran into Mr. Oliver, the custodian, dragging a bucket of water from the closet.

"Hey, girly!" He greeted, an immediate smile replacing the frown she'd been wearing since Duchess ran out of the house. "You a lil' behind ain't ya?" He straightened his back, one hand on the mop, the other on his hip.

"Yeah, Mr. Oliver. My cat ran out the house this morning. But I haven't seen you since school started. Where you been hiding?" Jada knew she should be getting to her class as quickly as possible, but she was already late. No need in sprinting to the lion's den if you know the lion's waiting on you.

Mr. Oliver shook his head, looking down at the mop absentmindedly. "Well, I been in the hospital. Doctors trying to see what's going on with my heart." Looking at him now, Jada could tell that he'd lost weight. She couldn't help but feel worried about him. After all, he had been her only confidant at Caldwin High last school year.

Sensing her somber mood, he attempted to speak more enthusiastically. "But, look here, ain't nothing gon' get this old man down. I been on this earth more years than most folks can count; I'm not out for the count just yet." He placed a hand on her shoulder for added reassurance. "Now, you need to be gettin' to class. Cause that new principal mane got it out for you, but remember that when it's all said and done, you don't have to answer to nobody but God and then yourself." He gave her a soft tap on the shoulder, tipped his hat at her, and strolled in the opposite direction, whistling and pushing the mop down Hall D.

Jada looked after him, amazed by how he could manage to sum up her life in just a few words. Even more impressive was the fact that he had no clue about the ordeals she'd been dealing with, but his advice still applied. *Thank you, God, for confirmation*, she whispered, looking up at the ceiling. Her heels clicked against the tile until she was standing at her classroom door. She exhaled slowly and opened the door. The entire class seemed to sigh upon seeing her; Ms. Calloway strolled from the back of the class, a sinister grin plastered on her face.

"Look what the cat drug in," she drawled. "Looks like you're gonna get that write-up after all," she whispered before stepping around Jada and exiting the room.

"Maanne, Ms. H, where you been?" Adrian asked, his arms raised with inquisition.

Reaching her desk, Jada placed her bag in the chair and pulled out her attendance book before walking back to the front podium. "Sorry, guys. My cat ran out the house today, and it took me forever to find her. I told y'all that she's boy crazy." She could hear the students laughing at her comment. It hadn't been the first time that she'd discussed Duchess's antics.

Adrian's face relaxed with what Jada assumed was understanding. "Yeah, a'ight. But you think you can avoid that next time? Cause ole girl, Ms. Calhoun, or whatever her name is, gotta bad attitude. We came in, sat down, and started on the bellringer and everything, but she just started doin' too much." Jada wished she could offer her own experience with Ms. Calloway to assure him that she understood, but she remained silent.

"You said the same thing about me, Adrian." She feigned thoughtfulness while holding her chin between her thumb and index finger. The rest of the students began to laugh, agreeing with her.

"Ah, yeah. You do too much, too, sometimes." He grinned. "But you a'ight with me now." For a short second, he seemed to lower his eyes shyly, but the expression quickly dissipated. "Ay, ay, but are we about to keep talking about your cat or nah?"

Jada laughed and pulled a stack of papers from her gradebook. "Last unit, we discussed power and you all wrote *very short* literary analysis essays. Today, we're going to start yet another unit devoted to power and politics, and by the end of the unit, you will submit a full research project that'll be due the Friday before Thanksgiving break." Moans echoed around the room, as she distributed the handout outlining the unit goals, essential questions, reading assignments, and final performance task. "Y'all don't have to sound so depr—" Her cellphone chimed loudly in her pocket. She silently kicked herself for forgetting to silence it. Fumbling to lower the volume, she read the notification on the screen; it was an email from Mr. Luther with the subject line: DISCIPLINARY REPRIMAND FOR TARDINESS.

Jada blinked excessively, sure that she had misread the message. To her dismay, the subject line didn't change. *Why would he send me this kind of message now?* She asked herself. None of his actions made sense. He may have a doctorate degree, but he didn't seem to have common sense. Sending her an email about a tardy without having the appropriate conversation seemed rash. On top of that, it was still first period, which meant that he had made this email a top priority. *What is he hoping to gain from this? Why would he send this while I'm in class?* She wondered.

"Yo! Ms. H!" Yasmine yelled from the back of the room. "I didn't get one of those sheets."

Jada ran her hand through her hair. "I'm sorry, Yasmine." She passed a sheet of paper down the row before slipping her phone in her pocket. Jada wanted to throw the whole day away; it couldn't possibly get much worse. Just when she thought that she'd gained some footing, it seemed that she couldn't avoid the blows attacking her right now. It seemed that Ms. Calloway, Mr. Luther, and even Cupid were against her. Snapping out of her reverie, she looked up at the students who were looking back at her in confusion.

"So, let's review last unit and the concept of power," she feigned excitement and reached for a dry-erase marker.

∙∙

Jada's head popped up from the computer screen at the sound of three raps on her classroom door. She smiled upon seeing Vanessa and Demetria sticking their heads into the room. Now, that she was teaching the seniors, she rarely had time to see her former freshman, except for in passing.

"Come on in, ladies," she called, logging out of her computer and rolling away from her desk.

They sauntered into the room, both smiling from ear-to-ear. She couldn't have picked a better pair to form a friendship. As a result of her mother's passing, Demetria had developed a nurturing spirit, which could definitely benefit Vanessa, who lacked proper guidance and, also, needed someone to confide in. As long as they didn't become heavily dependent on each other, Jada could certainly see them motivating each other in a positive way.

"So, to what do I owe the honor?" Jada asked, folding her hands in her lap and looking from one girl to the other.

"Well," Vanessa started, looking at Demetria for support before continuing. "We would like your help with something." They exchanged looks before Demetria pulled a slip of paper from a manila folder and extended it to Jada.

Jada accepted the paper and quickly looked over it. "What's this?" She asked, hoping they'd clue her in on just how she could help with Colorguard, which was at the top of the paper.

Vanessa began to speak but was stopped by Demetria's hand on her arm. "Well, you know that we have both suffered huge losses in our lives, and so, we are really looking to get more involved in school." She paused, as if assessing Jada's reaction. "We were both members of the Colorguard team in middle school, and the band doesn't have one here. We talked to the principal, and he said that we need an advisor and choreographer. So, we were wondering—" They flashed girly smiles and pleading eyes at Jada.

"Wait," Jada leaned back in her chair. "So, you want *me* to be the Colorguard advisor? But why me?" she asked, staring back at them in confusion.

"Demetria remembered you mentioning that you were on the Colorguard team in high school," Vanessa offered.

Jada inwardly kicked herself for talking so much. "Look, I would love to, but I'm already involved in so much right now. I'm sorry." She handed the paper back to Demetria, who took it hesitantly.

"Man, come on, Ms. Harris," Vanessa pleaded, her eyes growing red and teary by the second. "I need something that will occupy my mind. Please?"

Jada exhaled loudly, leaning forward on her knees and then back against the straight-back chair, which was becoming more and more uncomfortable. She glanced at the girls out of the corner of her eye while biting her inner jaw. She knew she would regret this. "Okay, I will help you, but don't you need at least ten members in order to make it active again?" Jada felt some of the pressure sliding off her shoulders. Surely, this would buy her some time, at least enough to dump it on someone else.

Demetria quickly pulled another sheet of paper out the folder. Jada looked at the signatures carefully placed on each line before looking back up at the girls in surprise.

Vanessa smiled. "We decided to go ahead and get signatures from girls who are interested, and that's only twelve. We stopped passing the sheet around once we'd gotten the number we needed." The two girls exchanged glances, clearly proud of themselves.

Jada gawked at them. She hadn't expected them to be so prepared, but now, she didn't have any real excuse not to help them. As much as she wanted to refuse, she knew that they both wanted and needed to belong to a group. Ever since she'd become the Beta club advisor, both Demetria and Vanessa were eager to help her, even though they weren't members. They had showed up religiously, decorating tables and even running small errands for her. She knew she would probably regret it, but she couldn't say no.

"Okay," she said slapping her thighs. "I'll be the advisor and choreographer, but understand that I am being pulled in many directions so I can only devote one day per week to you. We will discuss and make decisions on those days. So, as co-captains, you will need to get the band music on a cd." The girls pulled out small notebooks, taking notes. Jada instantly felt that she had made the right decision. "Then, we will hold an official interest meeting so that you can get people officially signed up and explain the obligations and stuff. After that, we will hold practice. The first practice will only be the two of you so that I can teach you the choreography. Then, the whole-group practice. Got it?"

"Got it!" Both girls said enthusiastically, closing their notebooks and jumping up from their seats. "Thank you so much, Ms. Harris!" They walked hurriedly out of the room, chattering non-stop about their plans.

Jada shook her head before rolling back to her desk. She grabbed the growing stack of student papers from the corner of her desk. Groaning, she quickly realized how far behind she'd gotten on her grading. She glanced at the time at the bottom of her computer screen; she had approximately thirty minutes left in her planning period. She could definitely knock out some grading, at least enough to give the last three periods their assignments back. Grabbing her purple pen, she prepared to focus on the ineligible writing scrawled over the first sheet of paper.

"Ms. Harris?" Ms. Allen's raspy voice sounded

loudly over the intercom. "You're still on your planning, right?"

Jada rolled her eyes and flicked the pen onto the desk. She would never get through the first assignment, let alone the entire stack. "Yes, ma'am," she drawled, leaning back in the chair.

"Mr. Luther would like for you to come to his office immediately."

Jada instantly sat up. She had already had enough of Mr. Luther for one day, and she definitely didn't feel like walking to his office, just so that he could badger her about signing the reprimand form. She knew he'd been itching to get her to sign the last one, and she was kicking herself for giving him something else to use against her. But she'd sign it, and after that, he'd have to grovel to catch her off her game again. Grabbing her bag, she marched to the door.

Chapter Twelve

Jada pulled into her mother's winding driveway. Feelings of guilt settled in the pit of her stomach as she silenced the engine and unbuckled her seatbelt. She hadn't been back to her mother's home since Caleb had shown up unannounced, and even worse, she'd been terribly distracted every time her family had called. She wasn't exactly sure why she was avoiding them, but she knew that she couldn't do it much longer. Just pulling into her mother's driveway made her feel calmer than she'd felt in the past few weeks.

She reached over to grab her purse from the passenger seat, pulling out the yellow reprimand sheets she had angrily tucked in the crevice between the console and the seat. She'd expected to get the third degree about being tardy, which she'd received, but the latter parts of the meeting had astounded her. She'd found herself face-to-face with an additional reprimand form and a glowering Ms. Calloway. Jada threw both forms on the floor, snatched up her purse, and marched to her mother's door.

Just as she'd inserted her key, the door swung open. Her sister Cara was staring back at her expectantly with her arms crossed over her chest. "So, the only reason you came is for Ma, and she's not here."

Jada stepped back to pull open the glass door. She'd briefly spoken to Cara a few days ago, and she hadn't expected her to be here. She, also, didn't expect Cara, the nonchalant one, to be giving her a hard time right now. "Hi to you, too, Cara. When is Mama coming back?" She stepped over the threshold, as Cara stepped aside hesitantly, her hand still on the door handle.

"I don't know when she'll be back. Maybe you should call her." Cara shot her a dumbfounded look before sighing heavily and sauntering towards the living room.

Jada stared after her, sighing in defeat. "Yeah, you're right. I'll call her and just stop by when she's here." She turned towards the door.

"Jay!" Cara called after her. "You know that Mama isn't the only one who cares about you, right?"

Jada paused, her hand still on the glass door; she turned to look at Cara, whose eyes had softened, as she walked towards Jada.

"I know that I'm usually the mellow, nonchalant one, but I want to know what's going on with you. For you, I'll care about whatever is going on." She placed her hand on Jada's shoulder, offering her a warm and encouraging smile.

Jada found herself smiling back, as she released the door handle and strolled inside.

***

"So, let me get this right," Cara said, cutting the edges off her ham sandwich. "He not only wrote you up for being tardy because you were looking for that cat, but he wrote you up for not knowing that a student had liquor in his canister?" She screwed the top back on the jar of mayonnaise, placed two sandwich slices and chips on each plate, and joined Jada in their mother's living room.

"Yes, that's exactly what I'm saying." Jada accepted one of the plates, her stomach growling in anticipation. She hadn't realized that this would be her first meal of the day, a habit she had sworn to break.

Cara plopped down on the love seat across from Jada. "Okay, fine you were late. He can prove that. But the liquor thing is just—. Can he do that?" She bit into the sandwich, her eyes never leaving Jada.

Jada followed suit, stuffing a handful of chips in her mouth. Her stomach seemed to express gratitude, as she felt it relax. She held up a finger as she chewed, her sister waiting patiently, like always. That was the one thing that she couldn't take from Cara. Out of all of her siblings, Cara was by far the most patient and caring, even though she pretended like she wasn't. Everyone in the family knew the truth.

"I don't—," Jada took a sip of tea. "I don't think he can. I've got to look in my faculty handbook just to be sure, but I'm almost positive that there's nothing in there that relates to this situation. It's all so very absurd. They realized that the student's bottle was full of liquor during fourth period, but he's reprimanding me for failing to report it during first period. How was I supposed to know that, Cara?"

Cara paused just as she was about to take another bite from her sandwich. She sat her plate on the coffee table and moved to sit beside Jada, grabbing her hand almost instinctively. "Jada, don't beat yourself up over this. It is unrealistic for that man to think that you sit in each student's face every minute of every day. Other than obvious signs, there is no way that you could've known that he had liquor in his bottle. Plus, if he intends to discipline you for not knowing, he must also punish the student's second and third period teachers. So, stop worrying. Get the handbook. Read it and fight him on it." She squeezed Jada's hand.

Jada sighed, releasing a small chuckle. "You know," she said, turning towards her sister. "You're not the grinch that I'm used to." She squeezed her cheeks, knowing it would annoy Cara, who jumped up and moved back to the other couch.

"See, that's why I can't be sensitive with y'all. Everyone will think I'm getting soft, and I'm definitely not doing that." She picked up her plate and continued to eat, peeking up at Jada after each bit. "But anyway, are you gonna spill the beans about Caleb and ole boy because that's the *only* reason I've been calling you." She wriggled her eyes in amusement at Jada, who tossed a pillow in her direction. Cara caught it before it landed in her plate. "What else did you think I was calling for?" She laughed.

Jada joined her. "I don't know. Maybe to talk about your own love life?"

"Ewww," Cara drawled. "When I meet a guy worth my time, you'll be the first to know."

"And who will you tell after me?" Jada asked,

chuckling inwardly.

"Probably myself." They both laughed boisterously, knowing just how true her words were. Sobering, Cara continued. "Now, tell me what's going on with the Jada love triangle." She rolled her eyes dramatically.

Jada crossed her legs, her elbows resting atop the pillow sitting in her lap. "I don't know, Cara. I was so sure about Johnathan, but then, Caleb pops up, and now, I'm questioning everything."

"Are you sure that's how it happened?" Cara asked.

Jada cocked her head to the side in confusion. "How what happened?"

"Your questions about Johnathan. Are you sure that you only started having questions about him once Caleb showed up?"

Hmmm, that's a good question, Jada thought, her hands fidgeting in her lap. She looked up into Cara's expecting eyes. "Well, no, not exactly. I can't quite say that there is anything absolutely wrong with Johnathan, other than the fact that he just seems too perfect."

"Hmm, what do you mean by *perfect*? There's no such thing." Cara polished off the rest of her sandwich and sat her plate on the coffee table, swatting her hands to rid them of any debris.

"Well, he does everything right. I mean, he plans beautiful dates, listens to soulful music, believes in God, and he gives any and everyone the benefit of the doubt. Like, he's perfect, Cara. It's almost unattractive."

Cara cocked her head to the side with inquisition again. "Hmmm, you know, Jay, I kind of get that. I'm only hung up on the last part about him giving everyone the benefit of the doubt. Does he give *you* the benefit of the doubt?"

Jada's face must have registered shock because Cara stumbled to complete her thought.

"I-I'm just saying that if you're feeling like he's giving everyone else the benefit of the doubt, where exactly does that leave you?"

Jada slowly closed her gaping mouth. "You know what, Cara? That's exactly what I feel. When I vent to him about different people, he offers these picture-perfect answers, but none of them really take me into full consideration. He *doesn't* give me the benefit of the doubt. He looks at things through this righteous lens all the time that, quite frankly, makes me feel judged, not heard. And many times I'm so consumed with guilt that I don't really get to feel my own feelings with him. That's exactly what it is."

Cara beamed, clearly proud of her assessment. "And does Caleb make you feel like that, too?" Cara crossed her arms over her chest.

"N-no, never," Jada whispered.

"Then, Jay, what exactly are you waiting for? Mama said he came back in a suit and stuff, so it seems like he's working to better himself. So, once again, what are you waiting for?"

"Well," Jada scoffed. "Now, I'm waiting for a slice of

cheesecake." She pushed her plate towards Cara, who laughed, grabbed both of their plates, and jogged into the kitchen.

"Now, you're speaking my language!" Cara yelled, pulling open the refrigerator doors.

Now, if I can just figure out how to tackle this write-up, Jada thought, reclining in her mother's roomy recliner.

Chapter Thirteen

The leaves fluttered to the ground in bronze and auburn hues, and there was just the right amount of nip in the air. Now, that it was officially October, Jada was in her element. Her skin was even glowing more than usual. And despite the fact that she hadn't called Caleb or Johnathan since their little encounter, she felt rejuvenated. Even more, she had just formerly appealed the reprimand she'd received from Mr. Luther, and she was prepared to fight. As much as she hated to be wrong most times, she knew that this wasn't one of those moments. The circumstances had been far beyond her control, and she wouldn't take the blame for what she couldn't possibly know.

Walking from the teacher's lounge, she spotted Mr. Oliver, the school custodian, as he backed out of a classroom, his broom and dustpan in tow.

"Hey, there, Mr. Oliver!" Jada yelled after him. Unbeknownst to him, she'd been avoiding him lately, too. He had this way of reading her mind and offering insight on situations she was going through even when she hadn't told him anything about them. But lately, she hadn't felt up to it. After her conversation with Cara, she was seeing clearer now.

His whistling ceased instantly, as he sighted her rounding the corner. "Hey, young lady! You doin' alright?" He rested the broom against the wall, took his hat off, and smacked it against his thigh. Dust and dirt particles floated to the floor.

"Yeah, I'm doing good, Mr. Oliver. How you doin'?" She grabbed the broom and swept the residue into the dustpan before dumbing it into the garbage can.

"Oh, girl, you ain't gotta do that. I was gon' get it.

That's my job." He gently pulled the broom from her hands.

"Ah, it's alright. It's the least I could do." Jada swatted her hands over the garbage can.

"Naw, it ain't. The least you can do is let me know you alright. I ain't seen't you lately. You like a ghost. Everybody say they seen you but me." He rested his fists on both hips, staring back at Jada with that scolding stare that she hated. She immediately found herself retreating into the little girl she'd always been when it came to her elders.

"I know. I know. I've just been dealing with a lot, Mr. Oliver, but I got it together now. You can rest assured that you'll be seeing more of me."

His face relaxed, and he began to roll the garbage can towards Jada's hall. Jada walked alongside him. "Well, that's what I like to hear. You know, sometimes, you may feel small in whatever situation you goin' through. Your problem feel bigga' than you. You feel like David. All you got is a little ole pebble, and you tryin' to figure out how in the world you gonna kill dat big ole giant. You say a little prayer to

God, then you shoot that rock with all yo' might. When you open yo' eyes back up, the giant on the ground, and you ain't got no way of knowin' how he got there. You David, young lady." He stopped at his designated closet and offered Jada a reassuring smile.

"I hear you, Mr. Oliver. I'm going to shoot my rock."

"You betta," he opened the door slightly. "Otherwise, you ain't the young lady I know." He tipped his hat and disappeared behind the door.

***

Forcing her conversation with Mr. Oliver to the back of her mind, Jada rolled the laptop cart back towards the library. In every class, she'd been amazed that the students had never conducted thorough research before. She had anticipated some problems when it came to their understanding of databases and catalog searches, but they seemed completely bewildered. The diagnostic assessment she'd received from Ms. Calloway hadn't exposed many of the challenges that she'd encountered earlier today. *Yet another giant, Mr.*

Oliver. Thanks for the tip, she thought.

Peeking through the library door, she noticed that the lights were dim, which meant that after-school tutoring was officially over. Jada quietly pulled the door open and walked backwards into the library, pulling the cart along with her. The sound of hushed voices speaking in the distance halted her. She listened intently, sure that she'd heard a man's poor attempt to whisper. Inching in the direction of the voices, she looked around to make sure no one else was watching her. Being that she was near the books and all the students had left for the day, it was relatively dark in that section of the library, the only light streaming from the sitting area.

"You know, you really are a fine teacher," one voice whispered. "You are nothing like some of these other ones, so just keep up the good work," Mr. Luther drawled.

"Why, thank you. I know some of the teachers have been giving you a hard time." The other voiced joined in. Jada immediately recognized it as Mrs. Yancy, a veteran teacher who kept up more drama than a little bit. She'd been teaching at Caldwin High for over twenty years and refused to take any new teachers under her wing. Even though Jada couldn't understand why anyone would want to be under her influence in the first place.

"Yeah, some of them are more of a handful than others. The new teachers are crybabies, and some of the others can just disappear, if you ask me."

"I'm sorry to hear that, but you know I support you whole-heartedly."

Jada chuckled within herself, knowing that the only reason Mrs. Yancy ever supported anyone was when it benefitted her. Otherwise, she didn't care one way or another.

"I know. I'm just glad you're not like that Ms. Harris," he spat, his voice raising several octaves. Jada shrank back, surprised by the vehement outburst. If she had any doubt about his regards for her, he'd just confirmed them.

"Oh, yeah, she's a mouthy one. But time will teach

her more than enough lessons to shut her up for good. I can guarantee you that. I've seen a slew of them hot new teachers bounce their goofy behinds in this school, and then, they meet the right person, and they can't handle it. She's gonna fall in line. Just keep doing what you doin'."

"All I know is that I need more teachers like you. You're cotton; Ms. Harris is sandpaper. No one wants to rub up against sandpaper. Nobody. So, as long as you and the others aren't like her, we'll get through this school year."

Jada frowned. She'd couldn't believe that an administrator would discuss her in such a derogatory way, especially with another teacher. She quickly plugged up the laptop cart, left a quick note for the librarian, and slipped out of the door.

As she walked to her car, Mr. Luther's words ran through her mind. She hadn't expected to make friends or get along with everyone, but the last thing any new teacher wanted was to be strongly disliked by the school principal. Even worse, she'd begun the school year with an open mind about Mr. Luther, and she'd tried to like him. But with every turn, she'd been criticized, unfairly reprimanded, and now openly offended by him. He didn't want to like her, and even though Ms. Calloway played a major part in that, Jada didn't feel it was her job to make him see her as a hardworking, compassionate teacher. She refused to make him think that his opinion mattered in the least. Now, she was even more glad that she'd appealed the write-up. His reprimand wasn't for school accountability; it was personal. The very last thing she'd do was sit idly by and withstand mistreatment. Not today, not tomorrow, not ever.

She slid behind the steering wheel just as her phone began to buzz in the pocket of her sweater. It was Johnathan. She hugged the device to her chest before answering, her voice trembling as she spoke.

"Hi, Johnathan?"

"Wow, I didn't know how much I missed hearing your voice until just now." His voice was shaky, but silky, just as she'd remembered. Jada felt her resolve begin to melt.

"Yeah, it's good to hear from you, too."

"Look, Jada, since I saw you last time, I've had time to think—"

"Me, too," Jada interrupted. "I just w—"

"Please, just hear me out." He paused, before continuing, his voice just above a whisper. "I-I thought about it, and I realized that I shouldn't have showed up to your house unannounced like that. I know I probably looked crazy. And I realized later that your ex caught you off guard, too, by showing up. I-I just—when you tried to explain it to me, it felt like you'd already chosen him, and I really like you. Better yet, Jada, I've fallen in love with you. I knew it then, and I definitely know it now. I really hope you will give me another chance to show you."

Jada sat speechless. He'd said everything that Jada probably would've wanted to hear three weeks ago, but now, she knew who and what she wanted. No amount of words could change her mind.

"Johnathan, I thank you for sharing yourself with me.

The past few months with you have been magical, everything I'd wanted, but I recently realized that what I want isn't always what I need. I had to ask myself if your imperfections were perfect for me. Can I live with them? And even though you are an insanely great guy, you're just not great for me. So, I'm sorry. I hope you don't think I've led you on, or used you because that wasn't my intention. It's just that I realized perfect doesn't exist, and since it doesn't, it's best for me to find someone who completely gets and fits *me*."

The line was silent. "W-wow, I can't say that I understand, Jada, but I wish you the best."

Jada sighed heavily. *Even that is a perfect response,* she thought, hating the sound of defeat in his voice. "Thank you, and I wish the same for you, Johnathan. Bye."

The line went dead, and Jada rested her forehead on the steering wheel. Her shoulders began to convulse with laughter, as she gripped the leather. It was ironic that she'd prayed for the perfect guy, found him, and still wasn't satisfied. Suddenly, she straightened, looking at her phone. She had to call Caleb. Better yet, she needed to see him.

She quickly dialed his number, started the engine, and pulled out of the parking lot. The phone rang several times before she got his voicemail. She hung up and called again, only to get the same results. This time she left a voicemail: "Hi, Caleb. I have to see you. Call me when you get this message." She pulled her gold PT cruiser onto the highway, headed to Stockville, Caleb's hometown.

Chapter Fourteen

What are you doing, Jada? What are you doing? She
thought, tapping her fingers on the steering wheel with
anticipation, as she turned onto the dark and curvy, gravel
road leading to Caleb's old home. Jada had spent the past two
and a half hours questioning and talking to herself. Surely, he
would think that she was a mad woman for just showing up,
but once she'd been on the road for an hour, she'd felt that it
was too late to turn back. Even worse, he hadn't returned her
call. For all she knew, he could be at work, but she had to
take the chance. He'd driven all the way to her hometown to
express himself to her, the very least she could do was return
the favor. Right?

A speck of light through the trees silenced all of the voices in her head. Rounding the curve, she saw Caleb's small, brick home sitting atop the hill, the living room light on. Jada noticed his car sitting in the carport, which made her breath come in short, sporadic spurts.

"What will I say to him?" she wondered aloud. "Oh, hi, Caleb. I know it's almost 9 o'clock, but I just wanted to see you. Hi!" She snorted, as she pulled behind his car, cutting of her headlights, and killing the engine. "It's now or never, Jay," she whispered, crawling out of the car and closing her door carefully.

Her shoes crunched against the gravel, as she marched to the front door. Usually, his dog barked whenever someone arrived, but today, there was nothing. Jada looked in the animal's direction, only to see the mutt cowering against the doghouse. Jada shook her head and climbed the steps. She delivered three short taps to the door and stepped back when she heard the floor creaking with approaching footsteps.

The door opened, and a petite woman stood in the doorway, staring back at Jada in provocation. Jada immediately recognized her as Breanna Esters, Caleb's ex-girlfriend, who had made several attempts to worm her way back into Caleb's life. She was a short, brown-skin and curvy woman with bright red hair and long, fake eyelashes that made it difficult to see her eyes.

She stepped out onto the porch, closing the door behind her, and crossing her arms over her chest. "If it isn't little Miss Teacher." She slowly ran her tongue over her teeth, looking Jada up and down. "Caleb's in the shower." Her lips slid into a sly grin. She was beaming with pride, which made Jada cringe. Jada balled her fists up by her sides, praying away the urge she felt to inflict bodily harm on Caleb. Instead, she turned swiftly and walked back to her car, jerking the door open.

"I could've told you that he'd come running back to me! All the education in the world don't mean a thing when it comes to a chick like me! He'll always run back, little Miss

Teacher!" Breanna called. Jada stared her down before slamming the door closed and starting the engine. Backing out of the driveway, she was shocked to see Caleb widen the door, a bath towel draped casually about his hips. A distorted expression spread across his face upon seeing Jada. She stared at him pointedly before turning her attention back to the steering wheel, leaving Caleb running after her and choking on dust. Her car slid from left to right as she sped down the gravel road, her mind unable to fully digest what she'd just seen. She had to get back on the asphalt. She had to get home. She had to sleep. She had to forget. She had to.

***

The porch light cast a bright glow on the lawn, as she pulled into her grandmother's yard. Her eyes were tired and strained, her face tear-stained. She'd been crying since she'd reached the highway, and after barely avoiding a head-on collision with a deer, she'd realized that driving home was a risk that she couldn't afford right now. Sucking up her tears as much as possible, she'd called her grandmother, who lived forty-five minutes from Stockville, and made her aware that she'd be arriving soon. She'd ended the call, thankful, she had two days off for Fall Break, which she hoped would be enough time to clear her mind. She had sensed the worry in her grandmother's voice, but she couldn't bring herself to talk about it with anyone right now. She just wanted to sleep, to forget about the entire night.

Now, she unfolded her body from her car and leisurely walked up to the front door, where her grandmother stood waiting for her. She fell into her arms, gasping for air between an onslaught of tears. Her grandmother pulled her into the house, patted her hair, and whispered words of reassurance in her ear. Jada heard and unheard them all at once, the room spinning around her. Finally, her grandmother released her, locked the doors, and escorted Jada to her bedroom. Jada set on the edge of the bed, her eyes cloudy and aching as she looked around the room, knowing that she needed sleep but not knowing how to go about getting it. It seemed to be an elusive task at this point.

As if reading her mind, her grandmother helped her undress before pulling a roomy nightgown over her head. She, then, pulled back the comforter and grabbed Jada's hand, who looked up at her in bewilderment.

Her grandmother cupped her face and tucked her hair behind her ear. "Whatever it is will be alright in the morning," she whispered. "Now, crawl into bed and rest."

Jada nodded stiffly and crawled to the top of the bed, positioning herself beneath the comforter. Her grandmother pulled the covers up to her shoulders and kissed her softly on the cheek before flipping the light switch and gliding out of the room. Jada tucked a pillow under her chin, hoping to keep the tears at bay, but they sprang forward anyway. *It will be alright in the morning*, she thought. *Please, God, make it alright in the morning.*

***

The aromatic smell of apple smoked bacon rested in the air, stirring Jada out of her restless slumber. She rolled over to grab the phone resting at the edge of the mattress.

Only two of Caleb's phone calls had made it through, since she'd arrived at her grandmother's home. That was the beauty of being in the boondocks; she instantly lost cell service, which meant that her sleep went uninterrupted, and the roads were fairly quiet throughout the night. Right now, that was all she needed, some peace and quiet, at least enough to gather her thoughts. She rolled out of the bed slowly, looking up at the sound of feet treading across the hardwood floor.

"Good morning, Granny's baby. How'd you sleep?" Her grandmother asked, leaning in the doorway.

"I always sleep good here," Jada lied. "Thanks for letting me stay, Gran." Jada attempted to crack a smile.

Her grandmother waved off her words. "You ain't gotta thank me. Now, come on in the kitchen and eat." She turned to leave, humming as she walked. "Oh, and your mama called. She wants you to call her when you get the chance!" she yelled, just before she disappeared onto the porch.

Jada shook her head. She knew that her mom had probably been worried, especially because she hadn't told her she'd be going to Stockville and much less that she'd be at her grandmother's. She was thankful that her grandmother had spoken to her first; she'd be much calmer once Jada called her later. Jada shuffled into the kitchen, peeking under the tin pans covering each plate. Buttermilk biscuits, crunchy bacon, cheesy, scrambled eggs, and buttery grits wafted through Jada's nostrils making her stomach convulse with a long and loud rumble. She grabbed a plate and piled it high with food before walking out onto the enclosed porch and sitting beside her grandmother on the swing.

"Somebody's hungry," her grandmother chuckled.

Jada looked down at her plate and laughed. "*That* I am. I hadn't eaten since lunchtime yesterday." She stuffed a piece of bacon in her mouth and spread grape jelly on a biscuit.

"That can't be good, big girl," her grandmother whispered, pushing the swing backwards.

Jada folded her legs on the swing and settled the plate on her lap. She looked out into the yard that was covered in brown grass and flanked by pecan and pear trees. The leaves rustled as the wind blew, a low whistle sounding in the air. Jada closed her eyes and listened thoughtfully, hearing the winds and dogs barking in the distance. She swallowed slowly before reopening her eyes. She found her grandmother watching her closely.

"I don't know exactly what happened, but whatever it is will pass," she lightly patted Jada's hand.

"I know, Granny. I know." Jada stabbed her eggs and popped them in her mouth, watching a convertible blue Mustang pass by. The wind ran through the driver's hair, which blew wildly. Jada nodded her head and looked toward the sky. "Yes, Granny. This too shall pass." She squeezed her grandmother's hand before grabbing her phone and finding Caleb's contact information. Her thumb hovered above the delete button, as she said a short prayer. *God, I'm sorry for moving without you, but I thank you for allowing me to see*

the truth. Help me to move on. And when you send me what I
need, help me to recognize him and be good to him.

She sighed heavily and lowered her finger, releasing her breath when Caleb's name became a series of numbers. She remembered Mr. Oliver's words about David and Goliath. He'd been so sure that she was a fighter like David, but considering all of the battles she'd fought recently, it felt like she was running out of pebbles.

Chapter Fifteen

"Alright, ladies and gentleman, don't forget that your research presentations are due in two weeks, just before the Thanksgiving break!" Jada yelled, as the students filed out the room.

"Ms. Harris, I gotta question." Jada looked up from stacking the papers to find Rebecca, one of two white students in her second period class staring back at her with an annoyed expression on her face.

"Yes, Rebecca?" Jada asked, attempting to sweeten her voice. So far this year, Rebecca had been one of the most entitled students she'd encountered in the senior class, and it behooved Jada that so many of the students were willing to listen to her. While she was bright, she walked around with the unfounded opinion that respect and satisfactory grades should be handed to her. So, Jada knew that this question would not be pleasant.

The girl plastered on a fake smile. "It's about the research project thingy. Like, you had us do Summer reading before classes started this year, which none of our other teachers ever made us do. Like, since I read the books on that list, can't I just do my research project on one of those books? I mean, the stuff we're reading now is cool and all, but I'd much rather do it on one of those books."

There's that fake smile again, Jada thought. "Well, Rebecca, I'm glad that you're enjoying the text that we just finished, but you all completed the reading journals for the Summer reading. We discussed them, and we've moved on. The purpose of the research project is to see your growth, and this text allows you sufficient room to do that. So, unfortunately, I cannot allow you to do it on those books." Jada gave her a firm look followed by a small smile, hoping the girl would get the hint.

"Well, I'm considering talking to Principal Luther about it. I just think that you're making your class harder than it has to be. I've never received grades this low, and on top of that, you give a lot of assignments. And you know better than anyone else that Beta club takes up much of my time. I'm just asking you to work with me." She flipped her blonde, wavy hair over her shoulder and fluttered her eyelashes with impatience. There was a twinkle in her sky, blue eyes.

Jada shook her head while gathering sheets of paper in her arms. "Rebecca, if you feel that talking with Mr. Luther will ease your discomfort, I encourage you to do so. Also, remember that when it comes to Beta club, you only have to obtain a certain number of community service hours each semester, which you have already reached. Any events that you attend now are voluntary. If at any time you have difficulty with the research assignment, please stop by during tutoring hours, and I will be sure to help you." Jada offered a smirk of her own and walked back to her desk.

The obviously dissatisfied girl marched out the room, her face a bright red. Jada was sure that it wouldn't be the last time she'd approach her about this. Jada shook her head, hoping to clear the exchange from her mind. She began to ruffle through the homework she'd collected; the stack of papers was rather thin, considering she had thirty-five students in last periods class. Frustrated, she threw the papers on her desk and leaned back in her chair.

She'd called parents, scheduled conferences, and even sent home progress reports, but it seemed that the students still weren't taking the homework assignments serious, even though they largely impacted their grades. Several times, she had held one-on-one conferences with students and found that they hadn't been assigned homework in English since middle school. Even worse, most of them were under the impression that they would pass regardless of grades, simply because Caldwin High couldn't afford poor ratings or additional drama. Apparently, this cloud had hung over the school for years.

Even worse, when Superintendent Greer showed up, the students all referred to him by his first name, and he seemed to walk on eggshells when it came to correcting them. So, even though class sessions seemed to go smoothly, Jada felt that her impact was limited; it was clear that the seniors, especially, had the administrators in their back pockets.

***

"So, yeah, Rebecca told us about the little conversation y'all had yesterday, and we want to do our projects on the summer reading books, too!" Tamiya yelled from the back of the classroom.

"Excuse me?" Jada asked, one eyebrow raised as she looked at a grinning Rebecca. "I think Miss. McAdams misinterpreted our conversation. No one will be doing their work on the summer books." She returned to writing the lesson's focal question on the board.

"If that's what we wanna do it on, that's just what we

wanna do it on!" The girl yelled adamantly.

Jada lowered her dry-erase marker while counting in her head. *Keep calm, Jada*, she thought repeatedly. She wasn't sure what had made Tamiya, of all people, attempt to strong arm her, especially considering that she was, also, a member of the Beta club and had been one of Jada's most helpful and kind students. Surely, something had to have influenced her.

"Like I said to Rebecca and I'm now saying to you and the whole class, you are not allowed to do your projects on the summer reading assignments. Let's also be clear that many of you plagiarized in your journals for the summer reading. Let's also remember that we are moving forward. That is final."

"Why you gotta be so rude, though?!" One boy offered from the front row.

"We ain't neva had to do no research paper, mane!" another girl yelled.

"We should be able to do it on what we want!"

Someone else offered before the room became filled with loud chatter and complaints. Jada crossed her arms and waited patiently for them to settle down.

"How about we just take it to Principal Luther. He don't like her no way!" Tamiya yelled; the chattering quieted. They seemed to be in agreement. It dawned on Jada that Principal Luther's disdain for her was just as evident to everyone else as it was to her, and in this case, it gave them collateral. They were willing to challenge her because they knew that he wouldn't do anything about it. She lowered her head and stepped around the podium, pulling her body up to sit on the long wooden table positioned at the front of the class. She dragged her eyes across the room to stare into the eyes of each student.

Finally, she pointed at the colorful bulletin board in front of the classroom. "That board says that 'the only place where success comes before work is in the dictionary', and I put it there for a reason. You all are so entitled that to face any sort of challenge scares you; Most of you really believe

179

that you are ready for college, but you're not yet. I've taught college; I know. I, also, know that I wouldn't be here if I couldn't help you get prepared for both college and life after school. This is not a power struggle, and your threats to go to Principal Luther mean absolutely nothing to me." She attempted to hold in the tear that threatened to escape, but it fell against her will. "I'm sad that you all would rather fight me on an assignment rather than try to challenge yourselves. You rarely complete homework assignments, and you do the very bare minimum on classwork. I'm not even mad at you; I'm sad for you." She wiped her face and jumped off the table just as the bell sounded.

"We made her cry!" One boy yelled as he exited, he and the others laughing as they shuffled down the hall. Jada plopped into the chair and placed her head on her desk, not very sure what to do next. Her head popped up when she heard footsteps announcing someone's approach. It was Marcus, one of the seniors from her fifth period class. He stood in front of her lanky and tall, his brown hand holding a polished, red apple that he extended to her.

"Every year, I like to give my favorite teacher an apple. Thanks for everything, Ms. Harris."

Jada reluctantly reached for the apple, another tear escaping from her eye and rolling down her cheek. "Th-thank you, Marcus. I really needed this, especially from one of my favorite students." She attempted to smile while dabbing at her eyes with a Kleenex.

He offered her a goofy smile and strolled towards the door, stopping to glance back at her. "Last year, you used to speak to me in the halls even when you weren't my teacher. Then, you started asking me to help you with stuff. When I found out you'd be my teacher this year, I couldn't wait to be in your class. You're a good teacher, Ms. Harris." He patted the door frame and left just as quickly as he'd came. Jada placed the apple on the corner of her desk, finding her spirits slightly lifted. She wasn't sure how or if he had known just what she'd needed, but he had certainly showed up right on time. Jada looked at the apple again and smiled, patting her eyes with each fallen tear.

***

"Hey, girl. Hey!" Mr. Williams waved to her, as she slid into one of the lunch table seats.

"Hey, there, stranger!" Jada greeted, unpacking her lunch box.

"Oh, I ain't the stranger. Where you been?" He wriggled his eyebrows at her as he popped a grape in his mouth.

"I've been using my lunch to call parents. It seems to be the best way to get in contact with most of them. I can't get these kids to do homework assignments." She cut her peanut butter and jelly sandwich in half and took a hearty bite.

"Girl, I don't even give 'em homework, especially not to those seniors. They're some entitled little boogers. You know they run off a teacher every year. Right now, it looks like Mrs. Kadashe is on her last leg." He threw his eyes towards the lunchroom door. Jada watched a disheveled and red-faced Mrs. Kadashe walk towards them. Her red, puffy eyes made it clear that she'd been crying. She settled at the end of the table, isolating herself from the others and slowly unpacking her bag.

"She doesn't look too good," Jada whispered to Mr. Williams.

He smacked his lips and placed a forkful of potato salad between his teeth. "Look? Child, she's not doing good at all. Those kids are giving her a run for her money. Apparently, she's lost all control of her classes, and they make her cry every class period. She might as well be a substitute teacher." He stabbed another grape and plopped it in his mouth while eyeing the frail woman.

"I've been so wrapped up in my own stuff." She shook her head slowly. "I didn't even realize that she was struggling that bad. What's Principal Luther and Ms. Calloway doing about it? I mean, she has some pretty warped views of the students, but they can't just let her suffer like that."

"As far as I know, they've both visited her classes on several occasions to speak with the students, but that hasn't changed much." He leaned closer to Jada, lowering his voice. "Between me and you, they've decided to form a culture and climate committee, and they asked me to lead the charge. I want to invite you to be a part of it."

"A culture and climate committee?" Jada chuckled. "Why me and how will this help Mrs. Kadashe?"

"Well, the biggest issue here at Caldwin is the toxic culture and climate within the school. No one seems to be on the same page, and we have to get back centered on the students. I'm asking you because the students love you, and even the ones who seem to dislike you have a hard time hating you. You have good classroom management, and you're involved with student orgs on campus. We need your input." He pushed his glasses up on his nose. "I'm thinking that if we transform the culture and climate, we can work to impact classrooms like Mrs. Kadashe's, especially. Unfortunately, she's not the only new teacher having problems."

Jada nodded her head, still not very sure of the committee's charge, but since she was being invited to the table, she'd be willing to contribute, especially if it meant a more positive school environment. "Okay, I'll do it."

"Cool. The first meeting is tomorrow right after school." He jumped up, gathering his trash in his arms. "Toodles!" He waved his fingers at her before bouncing down the hall.

Jada turned her attention back to Mrs. Kadashe, whose shoulders sagged in defeat as she fiddled with the food on her plate. Sensing Jada's gaze, she looked in her direction. Jada offered a reassuring smile, which was met by a blank stare, the light Jada had seen at the beginning of the school year completely burned out.

The bell rang, and all the teachers and students gathered their belongings and moved in the direction of their respective classrooms. Jada dumped her trash in the garbage, turning and suddenly halting when her eyes fell on Mrs.

Kadashe, who was still seated at the table, a forlorn expression on her face. Her students hung around the lunchroom leisurely as their teacher remained immoveable.

The main office door opened abruptly as Jada approached the lunchroom door. Mr. Luther walked out briskly, stopping to shake students' hands. He, eventually, made his way to Mrs. Kadashe and leaned down to whisper something close to her ear. The woman looked up at him with tired eyes before standing slowly and walking in Jada's direction.

Jada quickly rounded the corner, not wanting her to know that she'd been watching and attempting to eavesdrop.

"Mrs. Kadashe, can you please round up your students?!" She heard Principal Luther yell in the distance.

Jada reached her classroom, her students lining the walls as they waited impatiently for her to unlock the door. She inserted her key in the lock and glanced over her shoulder, spotting Mrs. Kadashe give her keys to a student, as she strolled dazedly behind the group.

Chapter Sixteen

Jada stared at Caleb's message; she knew it would be the first of many that she'd receive today. He'd been texting and calling since the night Jada had popped up at his house, and she still didn't know what to say to him. The weekend when he'd showed up at her mother's house, talking about their future, and the ring played in her mind repeatedly. *Why go through all of that if you're just going to sleep with your ex?* Jada thought, shaking her head in frustration as she slipped the phone back into her pocket. She could care less if she never saw or spoke to him again.

She pushed open the meeting room door, a manila folder tucked in her arms. "Hi, Mrs. Hudson, It's really nice to meet you. I'm Ms.—"

"I know who you are," the woman spat, ignoring Jada's extended hand and assessing her from head to toe. "I just wanna know why you picking on my daughter." She looked at Jada over rhinestone-accented, red-tint glasses.

Jada cleared her throat and settled into one of the seats positioned beside Mr. Fulton, the assistant principal. He spoke calmly, "Mrs. Hudson—"

"It's *Ms.*," she corrected, her lips spreading into a seductive pout, as she crossed her legs slowly and leaned toward him.

Jada blinked repeatedly, resisting the urge to lower her head. Tamiya's face reddened with embarrassment.

"Okay, *Ms.* Hudson," he spoke loudly, a slight grin tugging at the corner of his lips. "We are meeting to discuss concerns you have about Ms. Harris and her relationship with Tamiya. Correct?"

The woman eyed Jada and nodded her head. Jada looked from her to Tamiya, who was working extremely hard to avoid eye contact with her.

Assistant Principal Fulton continued, "Can you tell me what problems you're having, Tamiya?" He pulled out a yellow notepad and clicked his pen.

Tamiya looked at her mother hesitantly, her eyes averting away from Jada's.

"Go on, Miya! Tell 'em what you told me!" Her mother yelled, slapping her elbow.

"Sh-she called us stupid and said we wouldn't go to college just because we wanted to do our research project on a different book. I-I don't think she really likes me." The girl's eyes were fastened to the table.

The principal jotted down notes on his pad. "Ms. Harris, do you remember having this conversation with the students?" He looked at her pointedly.

Jada swallowed firmly. "No, I do not. I did tell the students that they were not ready for college because of their sense of entitlement and failure to challenge themselves. I—"

"What kinda teacher would say something like that to

her students?!" The woman interrupted, uncrossing her legs and leaning onto the table.

"A teacher who is concerned with their success after high school," Jada said, returning the woman's stare. "Ms. Hudson, let me just say that I am here to help students like Tamiya be successful, but if she is going to complain every time I give an assignment or put forth little effort on all assignments, she is not helping herself."

"My child is smart!" The woman yelled. "She don't need you or anyone else to confirm that!"

"I get that," Jada offered. "But there is a level of respect that she and many of the students in her class must show to me as their teacher."

"Respect?!" She gawked. "You earn respect. You can't talk any kinda way to my child and expect to get respect!" She repositioned herself in the chair.

"I'm not sure what Tamiya told you exactly, but I have no problem with Tamiya. This is the very first time that I've even heard of this. Tamiya has stayed after school with me to make signs for Beta club events; she's even driven my car to make a run to the store. So, I don't know where any of this is coming from."

"So, now my child is a liar?!" She raised both hands.

"Yes, she is," Jada spoke softly.

The woman jumped out of her seat, leaning across the table towards Jada. She pointed her finger at the table as she spoke. "What you not gon' do is call my child a liar!"

"Ms. Harris, can you leave the room?" Mr. Fulton asked.

Jada looked at him incredulously. "I-I—"

He gave her a pointed look, before closing his notepad, and resting his chin on his interlaced fingers.

Jada stood from her chair and marched out the room, her temper flaring and blood boiling with humiliation and anger. *Why'd he ask her, of all people, to leave? Who does he think he is? He is rarely visible throughout the school day. Who still wears a jerry curl anyway?* Jada paced back and forth in front of the closed meeting door. She noticed Mrs.

Allen chuckling to herself. Jada halted her pacing, opting to lean up against the wall, her legs crossed at the ankle as she waited.

Finally, the door swung open and a grinning Tamiya and her mom strolled out of the room, purposefully ignoring Jada and thanking Mr. Fulton.

Jada rolled her eyes, as she watched them exit. Mr. Fulton followed shortly, his smile disappearing when he saw Jada's stern expression.

"Ms. Harris, come on in so that we can talk." He held the door open as she passed by.

Settled in a chair, Jada said, "I don't appreciate being asked to leave the room, Mr. Fulton. To me, it sent the message that I was in the wrong and that whatever solution you all came to didn't involve me. I do not like being treated like a child."

He held up his hands in protest. "Ms. Harris, in no way was I trying to exclude or belittle you. I just wanted to de-escalate the situation."

"And that could have been handled with me in the room. As a principal, you are trained to de-escalate situations. That does not involve stroking the ego of a deranged parent and giving the teacher guidelines to follow based on lies. That girl came in here and lied because she wanted her way. I don't feel supported at all!" She stood to leave.

"You think you're the only one who doesn't feel support here?!" He yelled, running his hand through his curls.

Jada paused, her hand resting on the door handle. She turned slowly, surprised to see his dejected form slumped over the table.

"You're not the only one who doesn't feel supported. I took this position under the impression that I would be head principal. The day that you all met Mr. Judge Luther is the same day that I met him and found out that *he'd* be head principal of Caldwin." His eyes searched her face for empathy.

Jada released the door handle. "So that's why you're always in your office?"

"Exactly," he nodded his head. "The man doesn't know what he's doing, but he has years on his side. I signed a vague contract that I couldn't get out of."

"I'm sorry to hear that but sitting in your office all day isn't the best way to show that you deserve the job. He's running this school further into the ground."

"Ms. Harris, when some things are out of your control, there's no reason to exert unnecessary energy to a dying cause. He's not going to turn this school around. No amount of committee establishments or meetings could do that as long as he is in charge. He has the entire school board behind him. And that's why I asked you to leave." He cleared his throat. "You were getting worked up about a situation that you can't change. It's a system. These students have the principal *and* the superintendent in their back pockets because the school can't afford anymore negative media exposure. Your best solution is to give 'em what they want and get through the year, like me." He leaned back in his chair, his pen resting between his lips.

Jada cracked open the door. "That is the saddest thing I've ever heard. I know there's a system in place, but I refuse to lower my expectations or sacrifice my integrity just to ward off illegitimate criticism. I will leave Caldwin before I allow *that* to happen. You should consider that." She flung the door open and stormed out the office, Ms. Allen watching her in awe.

***

Jada's phone buzzed with notification of the culture and climate survey that Mr. Williams had delivered to her inbox. Jada smirked and slipped the phone in her back pocket, remembering Principal Luther's face when he'd seen her walk into the culture and climate committee meeting. Disgust had been evident in the downward curl of his lips, and he had averted eye contact with her. He began to shift uncomfortably in his chair. Jada slid into a seat at one of the library tables, inwardly satisfied with his discomfort. Jada had sat that way for most of the meeting, her arms crossed, as she peered at him from time to time. Eventually, he had tired of her silence and assigned her to the committee discipline group.

"Why discipline?" Jada had asked, crossing her arms over her shoulder and lifting her chin with inquisition.

"Where else?" He'd replied with a snort.

"O—kay," Mr. Williams drawled, looking from Mr. Luther to her. "I think that—um—before we officially assign people to committees, we should assess the current culture and climate by surveying the faculty and staff." He looked around the room for reassurance. His suggestion was met with an array of nods and murmurs.

"Ooh, I think that's a fabulous idea," Jada agreed, smiling at Mr. Luther. "Surely Mr. Luther isn't afraid of a little faculty survey."

"Not at all," Principal Luther snapped, tapping the table. "Let's send it out."

Now, Jada was looking at the email with a smile on her face.

There were twenty-five questions, two of which were short response. She'd never liked surveys, but this one was different. She would take her time completing this one. And she would enjoy every second of it.

She pulled her gearshift into reverse and pulled out of the parking lot, loudly singing along with EnVogue as she steered onto the highway. *Yes,* she thought, shaking her head and smiling, '*Before you can read me, you gotta learn how to see me.*' And Mr. Luther would be *seeing* her very soon. She sped towards her mother's house, increasing the stereo volume.

Chapter Seventeen

"Jada, please pick up. It's Caleb—um—again." He spoke softly, sounding weak and defeated. "Um, I've been calling you since you saw—um—left my house that night, and I know that you don't want to talk to me. I just—"

Jada ended the voicemail recording and threw her cellphone onto the passenger seat. He'd called and text her religiously, and she still hadn't found the words to say to him. Quite frankly, she didn't feel that he deserved any of her attention; she wasn't the one who had popped up into his life while still sleeping with an ex. Talking to Caleb was the last thing on her list of things to do today. She had an impromptu faculty meeting to attend today, along with Colorguard practice, and a huge stack of papers to grade before tomorrow's class. She just couldn't afford to listen to Caleb's whining right now.

She pushed open the library door, finding herself engulfed in a sea of silence, at least thirty pairs of eyes shifting towards her as she nodded stiffly and slid into a chair positioned between Ms. Henson and Mr. Williams.

"Good, now that we're all here," Mr. Luther's voice boomed, as he stared at her. "I scheduled this meeting to discuss the survey results."

"Uh—Mr. Luther," Mr. Williams interrupted, holding up his index finger. "I-I organized the survey results into color-coded charts that will make it much easier for today's meeting." He beamed with pride, the glare in his glasses shining brightly.

"No need, Mr. Williams." The principal waved him off and perched onto a table. Jada could tell that he was steaming with anger from the perspiration that slid down his bald head. He cupped his elbow and rested his chin on his hand while speaking sternly. "I have looked over the results, and it seems to me that many of you took the opportunity to not only express every miniscule grievance you have but to do so in a petty and rather unprofessional manner." He paced back and forth in front of the room. "For example, many of you dislike my references to certain educational theorists and experts, but this is not my first time at the rodeo!" He yelled. "I have been superintendent and principal for years! I know what I'm doing!" He slammed his fist on the librarian's desk, who jumped at his sudden outburst.

He continued, "I am not here for you all to like me, but respect should be a given. You respect me, and I will respect you." He made a point to look in Jada's direction. "Now, I do want to open up the floor for you to openly express yourselves, and then, we will discuss how to go about solving the problems you may or may not have." He pulled up his pants legs and slowly lowered himself into a chair.

"Apathy," a voice whispered from the back of the

library.

Jada craned her neck to identify the speaker.

"Please speak up." Mr. Luther said in agitation, rubbing his head.

"Apathy!" Mrs. Kadashe offered in a strained voice. "Apathy is what we need from you and every other administrator in this school!" She stood slowly. Jada noticed that her eyes were bloodshot red, her hair messy about her head. "I am and have been struggling with classroom management since I have arrived, and no one, I mean no one except Ms. Harris, has expressed genuine concern with helping me." A fresh batch of tears began to spring from her eyes. "I'm drowning here, and no one seems to care." Mr. Williams pressed some Kleenex in her hands. She blew loudly into the tissues and returned to her seat.

"And what, Mrs. Kadashe, do you need from us?" Mr. Luther asked, standing and stuffing his hands in his pockets. "When we hired you, we assumed that you had received the proper training to handle the students here." He scratched his hand, offering her a look of feigned bewilderment.

The woman's mouth gaped open. "But shouldn't you as a principal offer additional professional development and training to assist your teachers? I don't understand how you can stand there with a smug look on your face when I'm telling you what I need!" Her voice shook with desperation, which startled Jada.

"I would ask if anyone else feels this way, but I think that many of you will jump on the bandwagon, which seems to be the flavor of the week," he mocked, nodding his head.

Mrs. Glenn, another new teacher, raised her hand. "I don't think you are really listening. She is not the only one who needs extra help." Her eyes shifted nervously from side to side. "But every time we have a concern, we are treated like neanderthals, like we're weak and stupid."

"Mrs. Glenn, let me make something very clear to you and everyone else." He looked around the room. "I am responsible for what I say and the information I give you. I am not responsible for *how* you receive it. That's a personal matter."

"Wow," Jada spoke, shaking her head with dismay.

"Oh, there we go. Ms. Harris, I knew you'd have something to say." He glared at her.

"Why distribute the survey if you're not actually going to use them to modify the school's toxic culture and climate? I just don't get it," Jada said.

"And I don't expect you to. You're still new here—"

"And you are, too." Jada reminded him.

He ignored her. "Many of you all's complaints can be addressed by making a personal attitude adjustment, which me and the administrators are willing to accept as our newest challenge."

"Wait," Jada chuckled, exchanging glances with Mr. Fulton. "So, your response to the survey results is to adjust *our* attitudes?"

"Exactly. The administrators will also be working to

change some things, as well, but many of the problems in this school have been fueled by toxic attitudes and undeserving superiority," Principal Luther retorted.

Jada snorted. His statement was ironic because at the beginning of school, that's exactly what she had felt about Mrs. Kadashe, and that had been the primary problem. But now, they were beyond being able to just name the issue. She needed practical methods for addressing behavioral and classroom management problems. Yet, it had been the administrators' very own toxic attitudes and superiority that kept them from helping her and many of the other new teachers.

Even now, the meeting had been spent berating the faculty rather than tackling the results head-on. Jada looked about the room, noticing the shoulders slumped over in defeat and exhaustion. She was tired of fighting by herself. No amount of feedback would resonate with this man; that much was clear to her, and from the looks of it, it was evident to everyone else as well. She leaned back into her chair, releasing a long sigh and tuning out the voices.

***

"So, yeah. That was terrible," Mr. Williams whispered, grabbing Jada's arm and steering her towards her classroom.

"Hmph. That's the understatement of the week," Jada snorted, unlocking the door as he followed her into the room.

"I actually like Mr. Luther, but that was a circus. Those teachers are losing their marbles." He sat in one of the desks, offering Jada a defeated look.

"I really don't know what to tell you; honestly, I don't have very much to say at this point." She threw her gradebook and a stack of student papers into her bag. "As soon as I can, I'm going to the house and forcing myself to forget this mess." She shut down her computer and strolled to the door.

"Well, I guess I better get going, too." He offered her a reassuring smile, before waving and exiting.

Jada closed the door behind her and inserted her key

in the lock, pausing when a sudden idea dawned on her. She quickly unlocked the door and jogged back to her desk, turning on the computer and printer. Once it was up and running, she scrolled through her files in search of a specific document. Upon finding it, she pressed the print button and smiled to herself as she stuffed the thick stack of papers in her bag and entered the gym for colorguard practice.

***

Walking to her car, she slowed her pace as she watched Mrs. Kadashe pull a wagon full of overstuffed boxes to her car. Jada shielded her eyes from the setting sun and looked on as the woman loaded her car. Jada could see numerous boxes piled into the woman's SUV. She then hoisted the wagon into the trunk, closed it, and looked in Jada's direction. Her eyes were sad and decided. She walked towards Jada slowly and extended her school keys to her. Jada looked at them and then back at the woman before enclosing them in her hand and nodding stiffly. The woman attempted a smile but failed.

"Thank you," she murmured, turning and strolling to her car. She started the engine and sped away, leaving Jada standing on the sidewalk and tucking the keys in her pocket. Jada had heard about teacher's quitting mid-year, and people usually spoke about them with such disgust, but in this moment, Jada was proud of the woman.

Chapter Eighteen

"So, today is the day!" Jada exclaimed excitedly, stuffing her hands in her sweater pockets and looking from face-to-face at her first period class. "Anyone want to volunteer to go first?" She grabbed her gradebook and rubric slips, positioning herself behind the podium.

Her question was met with silence, as the students attempted to avoid eye contact. She noticed that most of the desks were clear, except for a few textbooks.

"Okay, raise your hand if you completed the assignment," she instructed. Only ten hands raised, many of which were halfway in the air. "So that means that the other fifteen of you have nothing."

The students remained silent, many casting their eyes towards the ceiling.

"You all have had several formative assessments that helped me to see your progress towards completing the research project—So what is it? Do you all need more time?" She looked about the room.

"Yeah, yeah. That's what we need," a boy offered nonchalantly from the back of the room. "They ain't gon' let you fail us either way." He pulled his hood up snuggly around his ears.

Jada looked from one face to another. Even though she thought she had made significant strides with most of the students, even Adrian seemed relatively confident that he would not fail. He, like the many of the others, had not completed many assignments, and while they seemed regretful during conferences, their entitlement still remained. They had proved to be untouchable for years. Although Jada's intentions weren't to fail them, she knew that they would give her no choice, unless she worked non-stop to change it. She had to do something. She pulled her pencil from behind her ear and tapped the podium.

"Your research assignments were due today, but if you don't have it or need more time, I will give you the opportunity to submit it the Tuesday after Thanksgiving Break with no late penalty. If you have your project today, you can present it or wait until Tuesday. This is the only opportunity you all will have." She leaned forward on the podium.

"I'll go ahead and do mine," Jasmine said, raising her hand.

"Me, too!" Marcus yelled.

Jada exhaled loudly, plastering a smile on her face before turning the podium over to Jasmine and walking to her desk.

***

"Excuse me, Ms. Harris. Can I speak to you for a minute?" Mr. Luther asked, suddenly appearing in her doorway and interrupting one of the student presenters.

Jada squinted her eyes at him. "Um—Mr. Luther, can it wait? Calvin was just finishing his presentation."

"Now!" He barked.

Jada trembled with anger at his total disregard for professionalism. She excused herself and stalked to the door, the students watching closely.

Mr. Luther stopped her as she attempted to close the door. "Did I hear correctly that you gave the students a research project over Thanksgiving Break?" He crossed his arms over his chest and glared at her.

Jada glared back at the man towering above her. "I didn—," she attempted to explain.

"If you think that you will get more flies with vinegar that honey, you are sadly mistaken, Ms. Harris." He spat as he talked, which urged Jada to take several steps back. "You have no idea how many phone calls the school board has gotten about your rather ignorant decision to assign students work over the holidays."

"I do not appreciate you interrupting my class and

yelling at me in front of my students. You have no idea what you're talking about!" She hissed loudly.

"Do you or do you not have a research assignment due the Tuesday after Thanksgiving break?!"

"Yes, I do, bu——."

"That is all I needed to know!" He turned swiftly on his heels and marched down the hall, leaving Jada stewing with anger, which became humiliation as she turned towards her classroom. The door had been left open, and while some students looked on in pity, others seemed triumphant. She unclenched her fists and forced a smile onto her face.

She settled behind her desk. "Okay, Calvin, we were on the questions and answers portion." She made a mental note to put her plan in action. "Does anyone have any questions for Calvin?"

***

November 22, 2019

Greetings Superintendent Greer,

I hope this email finds you well. I am Jada Harris, the 12th grade English teacher at Caldwin High School. I, also, serve as the Beta Club sponsor, a Senior sponsor, the ACT prep instructor, and the Colorguard coach. It has been brought to my attention by Mr. Luther that there have been parent complaints about my instructional practices and decision-making. Therefore, I would like to schedule a meeting with you at your earliest convenience to discuss the culture and climate at Caldwin High School and my experience as a teacher. I look forward to your response.

Best Regards,

Jada Harris

Jada pushed the send button and leaned back in her chair. She wasn't sure what would come of this, but at least she was trying. Frankly, she was tired of fighting and defending herself. She was fed up with being humiliated and reprimanded for ridiculous things. She was even more frustrated with feeling that her work was in vain and held no value. If she lost this battle, it wouldn't happen without a fight.

Chapter Nineteen

"I'm thankful for all of you and your support." Jada exchanged glances with each member of her family as they sat in the living room. Their plates were perched on their laps, filled with candy yams, chicken and cornbread dressing, glazed ham, and macaroni and cheese.

"Aww," her sister Selena mocked, wiping an invisible tear from her face.

"Let's eat," her brother Julian said, licking his lips before digging into his plate. "And love you, too, Jada," he grumbled through a mouthful of food.

Jada shoved a forkful of dressing and cranberry sauce into her mouth, reflecting on how her family had rallied behind her when she'd relayed her recent encounters with the students and principals. They felt that she had made the best decision in writing to the superintendent and even expressed interest in legally pursuing the matter further, if she didn't get the response she was looking for. Jada had assured them that she would be okay and that God was on her side, which had calmed their worries.

Looking around, she realized that this was the feeling she missed when she was with Johnathan. He wanted everything to go right and according to plan, but here she was with her family, eating Thanksgiving dinner off paper plates while watching a movie. Of course, her mother had a beautiful glass table where they could eat, and she owned more delicate silverware than many people Jada had met. But all Jada wanted was this right here. Sitting in a room with the people she loved and enjoying each other's company, no matter how imperfect it might seem to everyone else.

Her phone began to buzz beside her. It was a text from Caleb, wishing her a Happy Thanksgiving. She started to delete his message but decided against it. She pressed the call button and escaped into her mother's bedroom.

"Hello?" He answered as if out of breath.

"Hi, Caleb. I received your message. I—"

"Jada, I'm so, so, so sorry. I—"

"I know," Jada interrupted. "I couldn't respond to your text and calls earlier because I really just didn't know what to say—"

"Ja—," he whispered.

"No, let me finish." She spoke firmly. "I didn't respond because I didn't know what to say, but at this point, I'm not mad. I'm sure. I'm sure that no amount of words could make me understand why you came back. I'm sure that I don't want to understand, and I'm sure that this—whatever this is—is over."

"Jada, pleas—," he whined.

"I'm also sure that none of your words can change my mind. This is me getting closure and moving on with my life. Maybe one day we can be friends, but right now, I need for you to leave me alone and move on, too."

The line was silent. "Well, okay, Jada." He spoke softly, surrendering to defeat.

Jada ended the call, clutching the phone close to her chest, as she allowed the reality of the phone call to sink in. Surprisingly, she felt no tears threatening to burst from her eyes. She felt, for a lack of better words, sure. Sure that she was single. Sure that a phase of her life had ended. Sure that she was okay. She turned off her phone, checked her appearance in her mother's floor-length mirror, and rejoined her family in the living room. She was sure that she wouldn't want to be any other place.

***

December 10, 2019

Ms. Harris, I will meet with you briefly on next Tuesday, December 17th at 9:45.

Thank you,

Superintendent Charles Greer

Jada read and re-read the superintendent's email response, carefully analyzing each part. She sensed his annoyance with her, and she knew she would have to carefully present the information she'd gathered. Jada felt chills ripple through her body with thoughts of ousting Mr. Luther and Ms. Calloway. She checked the manila folder she'd been purposefully carrying with her. All of the documents were still in place. She was ready to fight.

Chapter Twenty

Jada's mind had been reeling since Ms. Allen had informed her that Principal Luther would be sitting in on her meeting with the superintendent today. She wasn't afraid of him, and it wouldn't alter her approach in the least. However, she had hoped to speak with the superintendent alone so that she could present all the information to him without any interruptions. She knew that Mr. Luther wouldn't sit idly by and watch her dismantle the false pedestal he'd built for himself.

However, he would not discourage her; Jada had been waiting for this day since the October leaves began to fall, and she felt extremely prepared. Clutching the manila folder against her chest, she pictured his expression when she'd allow the printed emails and documents to dramatically fall onto the desk. There was no way the superintendent wouldn't listen to her once he saw them. She pushed open the front office door, and Ms. Allen, the receptionist, offered her a warm smile and a thumbs up. The woman's gesture didn't match the worried look in her eyes, but Jada couldn't let that deter her. She offered a stiff nod in her direction and continued to the larger room. Just before entering, she said a silent prayer: *God, please go with me in this meeting.* She gave the wooden door two firm taps, and it creaked open slowly.

She immediately noticed the tall, red-faced superintendent who she had seen occasionally lounging in the school cafeteria. He murmured a quick greeting before turning his attention back to Principal Judge Luther, as they continued their small talk about football. Jada waited patiently, allowing herself to wonder about his name. *Judge Luther*, she snorted inwardly. She was still very sure that his

Mama didn't give it to him. *If she did, Lucifer would've been a more appropriate choice*, she thought. When their eyes met, the fire and tension that flashed between them was undeniable. He nodded, cupped his hands beneath his chin, and leaned forward on the large, wooden desk. She settled into one of the uncomfortable, straight-back chairs adjacent to his desk and pulled her skirt down snuggly over her knees. She exhaled slowly before opening the folder and folding her hands in her lap. Their talking ceased, and the superintendent turned to her.

"I called this meeting," she started, clearing her throat. "Because I wanted to dis---."

"By the way, Luther, what you think about the track team?" Superintendent Greer interrupted before crossing his leg at the ankle and scrolling through his phone. "Oh, I'm sorry, Ms. Harris, you were saying?" He smirked at her.

Jada looked across the desk and into the eyes of a triumphant Principal Luther, and she instantly knew that scheduling this meeting had been a huge mistake. She fought the urge to bolt out of her chair and towards the door. Instead, she planted her feet firmly on the ground and straightened in her chair.

"I understand that neither of you want to be in this meeting, but I am a teacher here. So, my experience at this school matters. Whether you like it or not, I scheduled this meeting so you will listen to me." She looked from one man to another, waiting for any interruptions. There were none, so she proceeded. "I began teaching here with high hopes that I could be an asset for these students. It was a troublesome first semester, but I signed my contract to return thinking that this year would be different. Since Mr. Luther has been here, he has done nothing but bully, criticize, undermine, and openly humiliate the faculty and staff here." She watched as the principal's face contorted from one facial expression to another. He shifted uncomfortably in his seat. He seemed close to exploding.

Jada continued, "First, he attempted to issue me a warning slip for the noise level of my classroom. The students were actively learning, and he said that the teachers were upset about that, even though he'd originally waved it off. I refused to sign the form because I didn't feel that it warranted a reprimand. After that, he has been inappropriately approaching me on several occasions."

The superintendent held up his hand. "Ms. Harris, I hate to stop you, but from my understanding, it wasn't a write-up that he was asking you to sign. I don't see why signing it was so difficult for you." He offered her a dumbfounded expression while scratching his head.

Jada looked directly into his eyes. "Mr. Greer, I understand the process for a write-up. A warning only leads to an official write-up, and I refused to assist him in starting a paper trail for something so small. So, perhaps, you cannot understand it, but I stand on my decision not to sign that form. May I continue?"

"Sure," he waved her on.

"After that moment, which I later found to be fully suggested by Ms. Calloway, he wrote me up for being tardy.

I did sign that particular form because I was late that day."

"So, at this point, I'm not hearing any information to substantiate your strong claim that he acted inappropriately towards you," Superintendent Greer murmured. He pulled his phone out and began scrolling through it.

"Because it's not true," Mr. Luther said nonchalantly, leaning back in his chair.

"Should I leave and take my complaints to the school board or are you going to put your phone away and listen to me?" She closed the folder, suggesting her departure if he chose the former.

He hesitantly tucked his phone into his jacket pocket and folded his hands in his lap.

"Like I was saying, after the tardy reprimand, he attempted to write me up for not knowing that a student had liquor in his bottle. He only tried to write me up, not the second or third period teachers who, also, didn't know. I felt that he had unfairly singled me out, so I refused to sign that form as well. Later, I walked into the library and overheard him speaking to another teacher about me. He said that I was sandpaper, meaning that no one would want to come in contact with me." She noticed a look of surprise pass over Principal Luther's face. Clearly, he hadn't expected her to bring that particular moment up, after all she had been eavesdropping.

"I said no such thing!" He asserted forcefully. "She's lying!"

The superintendent held up his finger to silence him. "Ms. Harris, if he said that, he was simply stating his opinion. He is allowed an opinion, even if you don't like it."

She shook her head, an astounded look on her face. "So, it's okay for your school principal to negatively speak about one teacher to another teacher?"

He readjusted his suit jacket. "What I'm saying is that regardless of who he may have spoken to, if it's true, he has the right to an opinion."

"I hardly think that other people would consider that appropriate for the work environment. That kind of behavior can only taint the culture and climate, which he continued to do. Several new teachers asked him for additional help and professional development, and he refused to provide it. He even went so far as to approve the distribution of a culture and climate survey, but when the results came back, his answer was that the faculty needed to change."

"A culture and climate survey?" He raised his eyebrow, throwing the principal a questioning glance.

"Charles, it was a simple survey. Much of the feedback had nothing to do with the administration." For the first time, Principal Luther looked worried, and Jada relished in it.

"Is that right?" Jada smiled, opening the folder and pulling out a stack of stapled papers. "Here are the results from the survey. If you look at the open-ended responses, you'll see that many teachers wrote paragraphs, essays even, about the poor communication, lack of instructional feedback, and support from the administrators." She passed the stack of papers to him.

He began to flip through them quickly, looking up at the principal on several occasions. The superintendent, obviously, didn't like being blindsided.

"You can keep that copy. I've made several additional copies," Jada offered, refusing to look in the principal's direction. "Also, he barged into my classroom before Thanksgiving and reprimanded me for giving the students work over the Thanksgiving Break, but what he didn't know was that I actually gave the students an extension. The project was due the Friday before Thanksgiving break, but I gave them extra time."

"No, she didn't. She—".

"Look," the superintendent interrupted. "I get that you got all your paperwork and stuff, but the main point is that the school board and I have received several complaints from parents about you and your class. I hardly think that any of this addresses *those* concerns. Principal Luther has said nothing but nice things about you to these parents. He has defended you time and time again to board members. We just had a meeting the other day about your class, and now, I think that we are all in agreement when it comes to your future here at Caldwin High." He looked to the principal for confirmation.

Jada sat in shock, stunned into silence at his words. She swallowed then spoke, "So, what you're telling me is that regardless of what I say and my feelings, you all have already decided to disregard his poor behavior and make excuses for these students."

"The students are our customers, Ms. Harris. Our job is to keep them and their parents happy at all costs. Mr. Luther has supported you, whether you know it or not."

"What he's saying," Principal Luther hissed, "Is that as long as I am principal here and he is superintendent, you need to start looking for a place of employment for next year. You will never work in this school district again if I have anything to say about it. You are spiteful and malicious." His eyes shot daggers at her.

Jada looked back and forth between them, her mouth

hanging open as she blinked in disbelief. "This is your idea of support? This is how you allow your principal to speak to his teachers?" She cupped her hand over her mouth as the tears threatened to fall from her eyes.

It became overwhelmingly evident to her that Mr. Fulton had been right. This was a system deeply embedded in corruption and arm twisting. They didn't wish for teachers who challenged students; they wanted teachers who understood the code and simply passed students. They had undergone enough scrutiny in recent years, and they would do absolutely anything to enhance the false image they'd presented of the school. Jada snatched a piece of paper from the folder and pulled the pen from behind her ear.

"Here is my letter of resignation." She scribbled a simple statement onto the paper. "Effective immediately." She laid it on Principal Luther's desk and yanked open the door, just as the fourth period bell rang. Students filtered into the hallway, bumping into Jada as she made a direct line for her classroom. Reaching it, she passed a group of students waiting for her at the door. She unlocked the door as the students exchanged bewildered looks. Inside, she strolled to the back of her classroom, pulling out a box she kept neatly packed away under her desk. She tossed her folders and desk décor into the box without regard for order.

"Whoa. Ms. Harris, what are you doing?" Shelanda asked, pulling her headphones from around her neck and approaching the desk. "M-Ms. Harris, where are you going?"

The others seemed to become alarmed at the girl's high-pitched voice. They, also, gained interest in Jada's packing.

Jada threw her tape dispenser in the box and picked up her tote, turning towards their questioning eyes. "I'm sorry, guys, but I can no longer teach you. I'm really sorry." She marched out of the room and down the hall.

Ms. Calloway rounded the corner. Alarm registered in her eyes. "M-Ms. Harris, where are you going?" She whispered, falling in step with Jada as the students followed close behind them begging Jada to stay. "Ms. Harris, you can't leave," the woman hissed.

Jada stopped in her tracks. "I can't? This is exactly what you wanted. The only difference is that my leaving isn't a win for you. I refuse to stay in a place that disregards my feelings and devalues me as a teacher. There are already enough heartless people like you in this world." She readjusted the box in her arms and continued toward the exit, leaving Ms. Calloway with a blank stare in the middle of the hallway.

Jada pushed the open the double doors and stepped out into the brilliant sun. The students continued to follow her as she placed the items on the backseat of her car. Her phone continued to ring and chirp in her pocket.

"Ms. Harris, stop!" Kamesha yelled, grabbing her by the arm. "W-what are you doing? Where are you going? We'll do better. Please don't leave. Don't leave," the girl begged, tears streaming down her face.

Jada grabbed the girl's hand, unable to control her own emotions. "It's not you all. I promise. I cannot work for that principal or superintendent. I'm sorry." She pulled her arms out of the girl's grasp and jumped into her car. The students stepped away from the car, many of them crying as she pulled out of the parking lot.

***

Jada cracked open her eyes, which seemed to be glued shut from the immense number of tears she'd shed. Rolling over, she grabbed her phone. She had over fifty emails, an overwhelming amount of missed calls, and more than fifty text messages. One was from Mr. Williams:

Harris, please come back. These kids are a mess; Principal Luther had to hold a school-wide assembly because so many students were crying. Rethink this. Please.

Jada read message after message. But even as she cried, she felt more and more freedom. Going back would be a temporary fix. She couldn't. Hearing her doorbell ring, she slowly padded to the door. It was her mother.

"My baby." Her mother opened her arms, and Jada seemed to fall into them, a fresh set of tears escaping from her eyes. "It's okay. Come on and lay down." Her mother led her into her bedroom, never leaving her side as they crawled into her bed. She rested her head on her mother's lap, as she spoke to her soothingly. "It's okay to cry, Jada. You did the right thing. It may not feel like it right now, but you're okay."

"I don't feel any better than the other teachers who left," Jada mumbled.

"You're not the other teachers. You refused to compromise and sacrifice your beliefs. I'm so proud of you." Her mother kissed her wet cheek. "Do you know that? What you did today was brave, Jada. And don't you worry about getting a new job. With the way that God works, if you made the right decision, you'll have another job in no time. He just wants you to rest right now." She peered down at Jada closely before lightly bouncing her knee, sending Jada into a deep and peaceful sleep, one that she hadn't experienced since meeting Principal Luther.

Hours later, she awoke with a long stretch, finding

her cat Duchess staring back at her. Jada reached for her, and surprisingly, she walked towards her, curling up beside her hand. Jada thought that researchers might've been right when they said that pets could feel their owner's emotions. Duchess seemed to be offering her reassurance. Jada would take all that she could get. The sudden smell of something cooking prompted her to throw her legs to the side of the bed and head towards the kitchen. Just then, her phone began to light up. She flipped it over, finding an incoming call from a number she didn't recognize.

She snatched it up from the bed. "Hello?"

"Yes, is this Ms. Harris?" The voice was familiar to Jada, but she couldn't quite identify the speaker.

"Um, yes. Who's speaking?" Jada asked apprehensively.

"Hi, Ms. Harris. This is Mrs. Kimble—um—I, uh, used to work for Caldwin with you." The woman seemed at a loss for words. "I know this may seem weird for me to call," She paused.

"Um, yeah. Why *are* you calling?" Jada put the phone on speaker phone and ran into the kitchen, mouthing to her mother, who closed the oven door and moved closer to Jada so that she could hear better.

"Well, I'm the assistant principal at Penelope High, and I heard about you leaving Caldwin High today. I know that you're a great teacher, and I've already spoken to my principal about it. We'd like to offer you an English teaching position here at Penelope High, which will begin in January."

Jada pulled the phone away from her ear and stared at it. "Can I let you know within a few days?" Jada asked.

"Sure. You have my number." The woman ended the call.

Jada turned to her mother, who stood with her arms folded in front of her. "God sure does work fast!" her mother exclaimed, throwing her hands in the air. Jada laughed and joined her as they hooped and hollered around the living room. *He works fast, indeed,* she thought.

Epilogue

Jada re-read the seven-page grievance letter she'd emailed to the school board in hopes of being released from her contractual obligation to the school. She'd already visited the new school where she'd be employed and met the principal, but she couldn't officially start until the school board made a decision on her contract release. She fiddled with her fingers as she sat in the meeting room. Thirty minutes had passed, and they still hadn't brought up her contract.

The superintendent looked her way repeatedly, clearly unhappy that she'd decided to show up for the board meeting. In all his emails he'd offered his cellphone number and promised that he would call her with news about the board's decision. He'd been adamant that the board was aware of her grievances and that she didn't have to attend the meeting, which made Jada and her mother even more anxious to be there.

Finally, she heard her name come up in conversation, with the board unanimously deciding to void her contract. Jada heaved a long sigh of relief as the superintendent stood and gestured for her to leave. Jada exchanged glances with her mother and walked up to the officials seated around the table, all of whom were white men except for one.

"Hello, I'm Jada Harris," she greeted. "I thank you for releasing me from my contract, and I hope you are able to fulfill the requests I made in my letter to you all."

The superintendent jumped up suddenly, his face reddening. "Umm, Ms. Harris. That's quite alright. You have been released." He fidgeted nervously with his hands.

"What letter?" one of the younger board members asked, his eyebrows raised in confusion.

"Yes, what letter?" Another one inquired.

"I found your emails on the school website and sent a letter explaining why I left Caldwin High school so abruptly. Superintendent Greer informed me that you all had read and discussed it. At this point I'm waiting for the follow-up call I requested in the letter."

The men exchanged dumbfounded glances. "I'm sorry, Ms. Harris, but we haven't received an email from you."

Jada cocked her head to the side and grinned at the superintendent. "Well, if you will give me your email addresses, I will send it from my phone right now."

The men each pulled out cards and handed them to her. Jada looked in the superintendent's direction before grabbing her mother's arm and walking towards the door, both grinning from ear to ear.

***

"Ms. Harris, this is Erin Little, one of the school board members, and I wanted to call you to honor your request in the letter. I, also, want to let you know that when you forwarded it to us, it was the first time we had seen it. I speak for all of us when I say that we are truly sorry for what you went through at Caldwin. Our only regret is that you didn't come directly to us after your meeting."

Jada sat up in her bed. "At that point, Mr. Little, it seemed like meeting with you would be pointless. The superintendent made it clear that you all had already made a decision about my employment due to multiple parent complaints. He even went so far as to say that Principal Luther had defended me at several board members."

"Principal Luther? Ms. Harris, Principal Luther never attended any of our board meetings, and I'm not aware of more than one complaint about you or your class."

Jada blinked rapidly, sure that she was hearing him wrong. "W-what? Not many complaints?"

"No. We only had one, but it wasn't serious enough to bring to Mr. Luther or Charles. Neither were made aware of it."

"Wow, so they lied." Jada shook her head. "I appreciate you calling, Mr. Little, but the problems with Caldwin won't get fixed as long as Greer, Luther, and Calloway are in charge. And I guess Calloway isn't going anywhere as long as her brother is the assistant superintendent.

"I'm afraid not," he said. "However, Mr. Luther will not be with us next school year if that's any consolation."

"Hmph. And what about Superintendent Greer?" she asked.

He chuckled nervously. "Well, —er— he's my brother-in-law."

Tales of a First-Year Teacher Sequel

THE FALL

Words from the Author

Thank you for reading this novel and supporting me. It is an honor just to know that your eyes have graced these pages. I hope that Jada's experience resonates with you. I could find myself identifying with her in so many ways, but not just in a school context. Research has shown that school leadership is the most dominant factor as it relates to teacher retention and satisfaction. I unfoundedly assume that leadership matters in several capacities, whether it is a church setting or non-profit organization. Poor leadership has led many people astray, and oftentimes, we aren't granted safe spaces in which to discuss this rather common issue. My prayer is that this book will prompt, or act as a supplement to the conversation. Furthermore, I find it extremely important to explore the personal lives of today's professionals. Questions that you may use to guide your conversations or book club discussions are as follows:

1. What do you make of Jada's relationship with Johnathan?

2. What does Principal Luther's first meeting reveal about him and his leadership style?

3. Was Jada right to have lunch with Mrs. Glenn and Mrs. Kadashe, the two new teachers? What does this lunch reveal about Jada and the teachers?

4. Jada accepts Caleb's invitation to dinner. Was that a good idea?

5. Mr. Fulton is extremely unhappy. Should he remain at Caldwin?

6. Is Mr. Williams a friend or a foe?

7. Given what Jada discovers about Caleb, why did he come back for her?

8. Does Jada make the right decision in regard to her job?

9. What does the epilogue reveal?

10. Who is your most and least favorite character?

Where do you want Jada to go next in this series? For feedback /suggestions/questions, email: parkspublishingcompanyllc@gmail.com

ABOUT THE AUTHOR

Born in Chicago, IL, and raised in North Mississippi, J.D. Parks has been a strong advocate for social justice and education; she believes in providing safe spaces for those who are typically silenced such as minority people, students, and teachers. Hence, she enjoys exploring and combining the lived experiences of under-privileged and under-represented people in cross-genre fiction. J.D. has served as both a high school English teacher and college professor. When she's not writing, reading, or performing both simultaneously, she is relaxing with her family and sipping from a tall glass of strawberry lemonade.